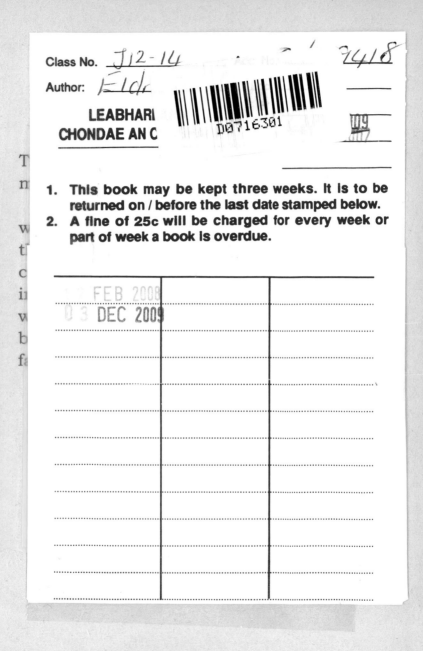

SECRET ASSAULT

J. ELDRIDGE

A fictional story
based on real-life events

PUFFIN

PUFFIN BOOKS

Published by the Penguin Group
Penguin Books Ltd, 80 Strand, London WC2R 0RL, England
Penguin Group (USA), Inc., 375 Hudson Street, New York, New York 10014, USA
Penguin Books Australia Ltd, 250 Camberwell Road, Camberwell, Victoria 3124, Australia
Penguin Books Canada Ltd, 10 Alcorn Avenue, Toronto, Ontario, Canada M4V 3B2
Penguin Books India (P) Ltd, 11 Community Centre, Panchsheel Park,
New Delhi – 110 017, India
Penguin Group (NZ), cnr Airborne and Rosedale Roads, Albany,
Auckland 1310, New Zealand
Penguin Books (South Africa) (Pty) Ltd, 24 Sturdee Avenue,
Rosebank 2196, South Africa

Penguin Books Ltd, Registered Offices: 80 Strand, London WC2R 0RL, England

www.penguin.com

First published 2004
1

Set in Bookman Old Style by Palimpsest Book Production Ltd, Polmont, Stirlingshire
Made and printed in England by Clays Ltd, St Ives plc

British Library Cataloguing in Publication Data
A CIP catalogue record for this book is available from the British Library

ISBN 0-141-31788-4

To my wife, Lynne

CONTENTS

THE HISTORY OF THE SAS

The SAS developed from the Commandos
of the British Army during the Second
World War. David Stirling was a lieutenant
in the Commandos fighting in the deserts
of North Africa in 1941. He believed that a
small group of men working covertly
behind enemy lines could have a
devastating effect on the enemy. His idea
was given official approval and so the
Special Air Service was born. The newly
formed SAS, just 65 men strong, carried
out its first operation in November 1941,
hitting enemy-held airfields on the North
African coast. Throughout 1941 and 1942
it worked with such effectiveness against
the German forces in the deserts of North
Africa that, in September 1942, the SAS
was raised to full regiment status, 1 SAS
Regiment – with a force of 650 men divided

into four combat squadrons: A, B, C (the Free French Squadron) and D (the SBS, or Special Boat Section).

In 1943 an additional regiment was formed – 2 SAS – and both regiments fought in the Allied invasion of Italy and Sicily in 1943. Then they took part in the D-Day landings of June 1944, again fighting behind enemy lines.

After the end of the Second World War, the SAS was disbanded. However, many ex-SAS men, who had seen the advantages of such a force, lobbied the War Office for its reinstatement as part of the British Army. The result was that, in 1947, an SAS unit, the Artists Rifles, was formed as part of the Territorial Army. Its official title was 21 SAS (Artists) TA, and many ex-SAS soldiers joined this new outfit. However, the military top brass reduced the SAS in size and importance. Many of the top brass did not like what they considered to be an 'unorthodox organization' within army ranks. By 1949 the SAS consisted of just two squadrons and a signals detachment.

Then, in 1950, came the Malaya conflict. Malaya had been under British control for many years. In 1948 Britain set up the

Federation of Malaya as a step towards independence. However, the minority Chinese population of Malaya, backed by Communist China, resented the domination of the federation by Malay people. Calling themselves the MRLA (the Malayan Races Liberation Army), they began a campaign against the British and Malays in Malaya. During 1950 the MRLA killed 344 civilians and 229 soldiers.

Mike Calvert had fought with Orde Wingate's Chindits behind enemy lines in the Burmese jungle in the Second World War. He had ended the war as Commander of the SAS, and he was given the task of reforming it into a fighting unit to deal with the MRLA. In 1950 Calvert set up a force known as the Malaya Scouts (SAS). This was made up of men from B Company 21 SAS, C Squadron from Rhodesia (now called Zimbabwe) and some reservists. In 1952 the Malaya Scouts became officially known as 22 SAS. 22 SAS fought so successfully behind enemy lines in the jungles of Malaya – living and working with the local peoples – that by 1956 the leaders of the MRLA had fled to Thailand. The Malaya campaign came to an end in 1960, with the SAS having proved itself and its techniques of covert operations.

The strategic structure of an SAS squadron had now been defined. An SAS squadron consists of 64 men in 16 four-man troops. Each four-man troop has to be able to operate independently, living off the local land. As well as being proficient in every kind of weapon and unarmed combat, the troop is capable of dealing with every possible medical emergency.

Further campaigns followed in which the SAS played a key role. In Aden and Borneo (1959–67) and in Oman (1970), SAS soldiers fought behind enemy lines – gaining the support of the local people and militia, blending into the scenery and attacking the enemy where least expected. During the 1970s and 1980s the SAS was a major player in the war against terrorism in Northern Ireland. In 1982 the SAS played an important role in the Falklands War, and in 1991 and 2003 in the Gulf Wars against Iraq.

Wherever war or terrorism threatens, the SAS is there.

Chapter 1
ICE AND GUNS

It was dark, and it was freezing. Subzero temperatures.

I lay flat on the ice-hard scrub and focused my night-vision glasses on the hut into which my mates Rob, Zed and Frog had gone three minutes earlier. Our intelligence guys had told us that eight of our people were being held prisoner inside the hut: four British scientists and four Royal Marines. The problem was that the hut was in a camp that was home to about 170 enemy Marines.

My name's Jerry Rudd and I'm a trooper with the SAS. I'm part of a unit of sixteen men which had been flown to this tiny island of South Georgia in the freezing South Atlantic. Our task was to recover it from a force of 200 Argentinian invaders. When we'd started our operation, twenty of our people were prisoners of the enemy. They'd been on the island at the time of the invasion.

In the short time we'd been on South Georgia we'd managed to capture one of the enemy posts, at a small harbour called Leith, plus their ice-breaker. We'd taken thirty enemy prisoners and freed twelve of their prisoners.

Now, we hoped, we were on the last stage of our mission to free the remaining eight. Twelve of us had set out on this final assault. Nine of us lay on the ice and waited for our three mates who'd gone into the Argentinian camp.

The Argentinians had taken over the British Antarctic Survey (or BAS) base at Grytviken, on the coast. The BAS base had originally been just a group of four huts. Now it was a fortified camp, with the huts surrounded by thirty tents. In turn, these were ringed by barbed wire and heavily armed machine-gun posts. Four men to a tent meant 120 Argentinian Marines. Add the men stationed in the huts – say another 50 – brought the number of enemy Marines up to 170.

Overshadowing the whole camp was the

enemy frigate moored in Grytviken's small harbour. This frigate was nearly 150 metres long, with a beam (its width) of 15 metres. It had a powerful array of weapons, including eight Harpoon anti-ship missiles, two six-tubed surface-to-air missile (SAM) launchers and a 4.5in gun. In addition, it bristled with heavy machine-guns and anti-aircraft guns. Also, beneath the water-line I knew it had two triple-tubed torpedo launchers. It usually carried a helicopter but, since we'd blown it to bits in an earlier attack, that particular piece of equipment had gone.

The reason I knew so much about the frigate was because it was an ex-British boat. The Argentinians had bought it, along with most of its fleet, from Britain. That's the trouble with selling weapons to an ally: one day that ally may turn into your enemy.

A frigate like the Argentinians' normally has a crew of 250. Add to them the 170 Marines on land, and we were facing odds of 420 to 12.

We had our own ship waiting offshore, HMS *Antrim*. The *Antrim* and the Argentinian frigate were pretty evenly matched. When it came to fire-power, the *Antrim* had two 4.5in guns, two 40-mm and two 20-mm guns – one large gun more than the Argentinian frigate. However, we all knew the *Antrim* had one major disadvantage: it couldn't fire at the frigate in case shells overshot into the enemy camp, harming our prisoners. This meant we had to release them before we could launch a major assault on the enemy camp at Grytviken.

Rob, Zed and Frog had done a great job, getting through the barbed-wire fence, round the camp and into the hut without being spotted. Since they'd been inside the hut for three minutes without the alarm being raised, we hoped this meant they'd overpowered the guards in it silently.

Me and the rest of our unit lay flat, our eyes fixed on the enemy camp. At this time of night most of the enemy would be fast asleep, but the soldiers in the machine-gun posts were wide awake. I could see them moving about through my night-glasses.

'Come on, Rob,' muttered Mack beside me. 'What's keeping you?'

Then we both stiffened as we saw a

movement from the prisoners' hut. The door opened and men came out, bent double. We counted them: 1 . . . 2 . . . 3 . . . 4 . . . 5 . . . 6 . . . 7 . . . 8 . . . 9 . . . 10. One short.

'Zed and Frog are at the front,' whispered Mack, concentrating his attention through his night-glasses on the activity by the hut.

'I can see them,' I whispered back.

Where's Rob? I wondered. Had something happened to him inside the hut?

Rob was our special pal, one-quarter of the unit with me, Mack and Jake. That's the way we work in the SAS, in teams of four. This operation involved three teams of four troopers. Rob, Zed and Frog were our best Spanish-speakers, so they had been chosen to go into the camp to carry out the rescue. In the SAS we're encouraged to learn at least one foreign language well enough to get by. I had some Spanish, but my speciality was Indian languages. I suppose that came from being a Fijian – or half-Fijian, half-English. Growing up on an island with a mixed population of Fijians, Indians and English, I'd got used to talking different languages.

Suddenly, through my glasses, I saw Rob come out of the hut and close the door behind him.

As I watched, the line of men dropped to the ground and began to crawl across the ice towards the hole in the perimeter fence cut by Rob and the others. Zed and Frog were at the front, Rob bringing up the rear, their rifles held ready for action if needed.

I turned my night-glasses back to the nearest enemy machine-gun post. All was quiet. Rob and the others had managed to get this far without any noise. I hoped that the enemy on watch duty were so muffled against the subzero temperature that they couldn't hear anything.

'They're going to make it,' hissed Mack, with a grin.

And then we heard a cracking noise. One of the prisoners must have broken the ice on top of a hollow in the uneven ground. From our position, it was only faint, but from inside the enemy camp it must have sounded really loud.

I saw the machine-gun in the nearest guard post swivel and start firing blindly all over the place, tracers of bullets hurtling through the darkness.

'That's it!' snapped Jake, on my other side. 'They need help!'

We opened fire, doing our best to pin down the machine-gunner and give our men cover. However, the alarm had been raised and all the other machine-gun posts had opened up.

I took a quick look through my night-glasses and saw that Frog and Zed and most of the prisoners were near the perimeter fence. Rob was pumping rounds at the machine-gun posts, providing covering fire so that the others could get away. As I watched, a burst of enemy gunfire hurled Rob backwards. He staggered, trying to regain his balance, and then he went down as more gunfire poured towards him.

I let my night-glasses drop and went into action, as did the other guys alongside me. With our guns blazing, we advanced on the barbed-wire fence, desperate to divert enemy gunfire away from the fallen figure of Rob.

While the others kept up their fire, I made for the hole in the fence.

Frog had got the eight prisoners through it and was hustling them away, urging them with shouts and thumps to keep their heads down. When he saw me arrive, he gestured backwards and held up two fingers. There was too much noise of gunfire for him to be able to use words. I nodded. I knew what Frog was telling me: two of our men were still inside the camp.

I clambered through the hole in the fence and found Zed trying to lift Rob up. Blood was seeping from Rob's left arm and right thigh.

I heard Rob mutter, 'Bad. Really bad.'

He knew he was losing blood fast.

'Under control, mate,' I reassured him.

Zed and I grabbed Rob and hauled him through the hole. Next we began fixing tourniquets round Rob's right thigh and his upper left arm to stop the bleeding. At this stage I didn't know if he was hit anywhere else.

The gun battle continued, firing coming from all directions.

Then Mack and Jake had joined us.

'Is he alive?' shouted Jake, just about making himself heard about the noise.

I nodded.

'OK,' said Mack. 'Let's get him out of here.'

As we got back to our own lines behind the ice-ridge overlooking the Argentinian camp, I heard our commanding officer, Captain Wilson, shout into his radio, *'OK, let 'em have it!'*

Knowing that everyone was clear, the guns of the *Antrim* began their bombardment of the Argentinian positions, raining heavy artillery down on their frigate and their camp.

From that moment, it was all over.

Within minutes the Argentinians stopped firing and started waving white sheets.

They were surrendering.

Chapter 2
THE WAR CONTINUES

Rob was lucky. OK, he'd been badly shot up, but he was alive. With proper medical attention, he'd recover.

Me, Mack and Jake went to see him in the sick-bay on the *Antrim* once he'd regained consciousness. The three of us looked an unlikely team. 'Mack' McGinniss was enormous, 6 feet 2 inches tall, built like a barrel on legs. He had a huge bush of red hair that fell down over his ears, like he was trying to hide under it, and his face was dominated by a massive walrus moustache, which was also red. I'd said to him once that when he woke up in the morning it must be like looking over a red hedge! When it came to camouflage, Mack was the hardest one to deal with; disguising him was virtually impossible.

Next to Mack, and dwarfed by him,

stood Jake Patterson. His hair close-cropped, Jake was the smallest member of our troop, at 5 feet 6 inches, but tough as nails. You could just see the tips of tattoos peeking out from his sleeves and his collar. When he was stripped he looked like an art gallery: tattoos all over.

Lastly, there was me: Jerry Rudd, twenty years old and one year in the SAS under my belt. I see myself as the quiet one of our troop. The thinker. Mind, that's not the opinion the others have: they tell me I talk too much! It's funny how other people see you very differently from how you see yourself.

Rob was propped up against a pillow, looking very groggy.

'What happened?' he asked.

'You took a bullet in your right thigh which broke your thigh-bone, and one in your left arm,' Mack told him. 'You're going to be out of action for a bit.'

'I remember that,' he said. 'I mean, what happened afterwards? I heard more gunfire and then explosions . . .'

'That was the *Antrim* firing,' I said. 'Once we'd got the prisoners out beyond the fence, Captain Wilson radioed the *Antrim* and . . . Wham! The *Antrim* went into action straight away. You should have seen it. When those big guns start firing they really have an impact. First they hit the Argentinian frigate, then they started on the camp.'

'We were lucky they didn't hit us,' said Rob.

'Accurate marksmanship,' said Jake.

'How are the rest of the guys?' asked Rob. 'Anyone else injured?'

I shook my head.

'No, you were our only casualty. The *Antrim* didn't have to keep up its bombardment for long. The Argentinians surrendered almost at once, coming out waving white sheets. That was it. End of story.'

'And now?'

'The Commandos and Marines are mopping up, taking prisoners and getting the mines lifted from the road. The rest of the task force from Britain are well on their way south. Aircraft-carriers. Destroyers. The works. Once they get here, you're going to be transferred to a proper hospital ship. Loads of lovely nurses making a fuss of you! They'll soon have you up and about.'

'And what about you lot?' asked Rob.

Mack grinned.

'For us poor souls, there's still work to do,' he said. 'No chance for us to lie around in bed all day like some people! We may have got South Georgia back from the Argentinians, but they're still in control of the Falkland Islands. So that's our next job: to kick them off the Falklands.'

As Mack had said, our victory on South Georgia had just been the start. And a small start at that.

To be honest, to me and the rest of our lads, the way this whole war had started seemed pretty stupid.

The Falklands were a bunch of small islands way down in the South Atlantic, about 500 kilometres off the coast of Argentina in South America. They had been British territory for about 150 years and were filled with a lot of sheep and very few people. South Georgia was ruled by the Falklands, even though it was not part of them. It was further south, nearer Antarctica. A piece of bare, frozen rock, it was inhabited by a British Antarctic Survey team of scientists and some birds.

For some reason, Argentina had been

claiming the Falklands for years, and talks had been going on between the British and Argentinian governments about the Argentinians becoming their rulers.

On Friday 19 March 1982, some Argentinian scrap-dealers had landed at the disused whaling-station at Leith on South Georgia and raised their country's flag. The British Government told them to take it down. The scrap-dealers refused. To make matters worse, the Argentinian Government sent an ice-breaker and a frigate to South Georgia. They carried soldiers and Marines to 'protect the scrap-dealers', as the Argentinians put it.

At the same time, the Argentinians had sent a huge, heavily armed force of army and air personnel to invade the Falkland Islands. The islanders were now their prisoners, surrounded by Argentinian army and air force bases.

The British Government responded by organizing an armed force of its own, which it had dispatched by sea. Britain is a long way from the Falklands and it was going to take weeks for this task force to arrive.

That was why we in the SAS had been

flown out. We had two jobs to do. One was to take back South Georgia Island. The second was to recce the situation on the Falklands and prepare the way for the main invasion force that was to recapture them from the enemy invaders.

We'd accomplished the first phase, so now we were on our way on the *Antrim* to the Falkland Islands for the next part of our mission.

Word had reached us that the task force was approaching the Falklands. It was formidable: two aircraft-carriers, a large assault ship, nine frigates and destroyers, plus various support ships, including tankers, container ships, hospital ships and repair ships. As well as thousands of soldiers, sailors and RAF personnel. It was like taking a large city to sea. But however big it was, it had several major dis-advantages. Firstly, it was trying to retake islands on which the enemy had become firmly entrenched. Secondly, the enemy were only 500 kilometres from their home bases, while the task force was thousands of kilometres from Britain. Finally, a ship at sea is a sitting target for aircraft.

* * *

19

On the second day of our journey north to the Falkland Islands, all of us SAS men were called into the *Antrim*'s briefing-room.

Captain Wilson was standing in front of a large map of the Falklands. It showed that they consisted of three large islands – West Falkland, East Falkland and Lafonia Island – with loads of much smaller ones dotted around them. The most important island was East Falkland, on which was Port Stanley, the capital. Captain Wilson had drawn a ring in red marker pen round one of the small islands.

'Gentlemen,' he said, tapping it with his finger, 'this is Pebble Island, your next target. It doesn't look much, nevertheless it has an airfield. The airfield was spotted by one of our Harriers which had picked up signals from its air-traffic control and early-warning radars. So, although we know the Argentinians have planes on the island, we don't know how many and what type. However, irrespective of their type, these enemy aircraft are a threat to our task force and, hence, the plans to retake the Falklands. We *have* to knock them out.'

'Couldn't one of our big ships just

bombard the island and wipe the enemy out? The planes, the airfield, the lot,' suggested Wiggy Jones.

'That would be an option, except for one thing,' replied Wilson. 'There are civilians living there. We can't risk their lives. No, I'm afraid there's only one way to do this. We need to get a recce party on to the island. It will report back on which houses are being used by civilians and which are being used by the Argentinians. Also, we need to know the number of planes and military personnel on the airfield and near by. In short, we want a thorough break-down of the situation on Pebble Island. We need as much information as you can gather so that we can mount a proper assault later.

'We'll be putting two troops on to the island under cover of darkness, at the furthest point from the airfield. They will be Troops 14 and 15.'

I sat up at this and looked across at Mack and Jake and grinned. The three of us were 14 Troop, which meant we were going to be right in at the start of the action. 15 Troop consisted of Banco Watts, Dobbs Dobson, Frog French and Mick McNulty.

'Rather than risk the enemy picking up your transmissions, you will maintain radio silence. You'll be inserted at twenty-one hundred hours and picked up twenty-four hours later at the same place.'

Wilson looked at the clock on the wall.

'We should be arriving off Pebble Island tomorrow, so Troops 14 and 15 will check their equipment over and then get some rest. You're going to have a busy time.'

Chapter 3
PEBBLE ISLAND

The Sea King helicopter lifted off the Antrim at 20.45 hours and was immediately hit by the strong wind. Inside, we all held on to something as the chopper was buffeted about. It didn't help that our pilot flew low to avoid radar, so that freezing cold spray from the South Atlantic's huge waves came in through the open doors. I looked at the angry ocean just below us and hoped that we wouldn't have to ditch. Even with our survival gear on, we wouldn't last long in these conditions.

At exactly 21.00 hours the Sea King reached the northern-most point of Pebble Island and hovered a metre above the ground while we jumped out on the frozen ground. Then it roared away, back to the *Antrim,* leaving us on our own.

We had two separate assignments. 15

Troop were to identify which of the houses contained British civilians and which had been taken over by the Argentinians. Our troop's mission was to try to estimate the enemy strength at the airfield itself, as well as the number and type of planes. But first we had to get from this isolated spot in the north of the island to the airfield down south without being seen.

Even though it wasn't as ice- and snow-covered as South Georgia, Pebble Island was similar in that it was a chunk of granite rock covered with bog and moss. No trees or hedges grew there, which made finding natural cover almost impossible.

'We're going to have to move by night. Get as far as we can, and then dig scrapes before dawn,' grunted Banco.

We all nodded. We'd already reached the same conclusion. A 'scrape' is a hole that you can pull a cover over and hide in. The trouble was, digging one on Pebble Island wasn't going to be easy. I'd already tested the ground and found that once you'd dug down about a quarter of a metre into the moss, you hit either granite or you went straight through to icy water.

'Maybe the digging will be easier nearer the airfield,' said Frog hopefully.

'Knowing my luck, it'll be worse,' groaned Jake. That was one thing you could be sure of with Jake: whatever the situation, he would find something to moan about.

We set off at as fast a pace as we could in the treacherous conditions. The rocky ground was uneven, full of deep crevasses and holes hidden by moss. Where the granite was exposed, a thin covering of ice made it slippery. There was also the freezing cold wind. On the positive side, this inhospitable environment probably meant that there wouldn't be enemy look-outs up here, in the northern part of Pebble Island.

It took us four hours of hard slog to cover the fifteen kilometres down south to the airfield. There were no lights on, presumably to protect it from night attack.

We laid ourselves down and put on night-goggles to survey the airfield and its surroundings. There was a small settlement of nine bungalows and one two-storey house about three kilometres away. We could also make out a large building, like a barn, near by. We'd been told this was the Wool Shed, where wool shorn from the sheep was stored.

Beside me, Mack shook his head in amazement.

'I can't believe that people actually want to live here,' he said. 'Think of all the places there are in the world. Places where there's sunshine. Australia. Hawaii. Fiji. Good heavens, we even get sunshine in Glasgow! But this place is the end of the world!'

'Maybe we're seeing it at a bad time,' I said.

'Not for me,' said Mack. 'I can't see any reason why people would want to come here.'

'I read about this Canadian couple,' put in Dobbs, 'who were so terrified of their kids being caught up in a nuclear war that they decided the safest place on the whole planet was the Falkland Islands. So a year ago they moved their whole family here. Now they're surrounded by ten thousand heavily armed Argentinian soldiers, with another twenty thousand of our blokes coming to fight them – accompanied by subs and ships with nuclear weapons. You've got to have a sense of humour to appreciate that, eh? Talk about out of the frying pan and into the fire.'

Satisfied that there was no one about, we moved slowly forwards. As 15 Troop headed over to the settlement of houses to start on their scrapes, me, Jake and Mack headed towards the airfield. When we reached a good observation point, we began digging our own scrapes. It proved to be just as difficult as it would have been up north.

By scraping away with our mini-shovels, we managed to get down to just over a quarter of a metre, making holes that were just long enough for each of us to lie down in. It was tempting to try and rearrange some of the rocks to build a hide, but the enemy might have noticed them. Instead Jake and I unrolled our sheets of hessian and spread them over our scrapes, and then piled moss and peat and grass on top of the hessian. From the air it would look just the same as the area surrounding it.

By the time dawn came up, all seven of us were concealed beneath our camouflaged hessian covers. Our scrapes had filled up with icy water, but there wasn't a lot we could do about it except endure it.

I trained my binoculars on the airfield. And airfield is what it was. There was just a small hut by the side of the rough runway, with some tents further back. From the number of tents, I calculated that there were about sixty men, at the most, based there. I reckoned they would be the aircraft mechanics and the soldiers to guard the airfield. I guessed that the officers and the pilots would be in more comfortable accommodation in the nearby houses. I wondered if there were any enemy housed inside the Wool Shed. I was sure 15 Troop would come up with that answer.

The fence surrounding the airfield was only about a metre high, just tall enough to keep sheep out. The Argentinians hadn't bothered to increase the height, nor to electrify it, which was good news for us.

I concentrated on the aircraft dotted around the airfield. I counted eight Pucara planes and four helicopters: three large assault Mil Mi-24s and a smaller Alouette.

The Pucara was a twin turbo-prop assault aircraft. It had a maximum speed of 500 km/h, a range of 3,042 kilometres and two 20-mm cannon and four machine-guns as armament. It would have a devastating effect on any troops attempting landing from the sea, which was the only way we would be able to retake the Falklands. The four choppers also had formidable fire-power between them: the Mi-24s each had a four-barrel machine-gun in the nose, plus four rocket-launchers; while the Alouette could carry four SAMs.

I caught a glimpse of movement out of the corner of my eye, and then the large figure of Mack joined me. He was covered with moss and grass to give him perfect camouflage.

'Tempting, eh, Jerry?' he said with a grin, gesturing towards the airfield. 'We could knock those planes out between us. No problem!'

'May be, but our orders are just to observe,' I said. 'We do nothing to alarm the enemy. And don't forget, there are civilians here too. British civilians. We daren't do anything that could get them caught in the cross-fire.'

'True,' said Mack. 'Anyway, I thought I'd work my way round to the other side of the airfield and see what the Argentinians are hiding there.'

'Be careful,' I said.

'I always am,' said Mack.

With that, he snaked across the bog on

elbows and knees, his camouflaged rifle always at the ready.

I turned back to watching the airfield through my binoculars. Lying full-length in my wet scrape was horrible and, as the hours went past, boring. But, then, most observation work usually is. You have to sit or lie and watch for hour after hour, sometimes for days on end. Gradually you build up a picture of the enemy: their strengths; their weak points; their routines, like when they change guards or have meals; how many are on guard at any one time, and at which points. 'Know your enemy' is the first rule of warfare. And not just know a little bit about them: if you are going to be able to defeat them, you have to know as much as possible about them, especially their weaknesses. Then, when you strike, it is at their weakest points.

I spent the rest of the day watching and making shorthand notes of when the guards were changed and when the aircraft were worked on.

At one point the small Alouette chopper went up to circle over Pebble Island. I guessed it was carrying out a routine observation mission, because there didn't seem to be any urgency accompanying its take-off. The whole time the Alouette was buzzing around, me and all the other blokes kept as still as we could beneath our camouflaged covers.

Dusk began to fall at about 16.00 hours. We immediately began clearing the camouflage off our hessian covers and packing them up, prior to starting back to the rendezvous, or RV. That's another rule on an observation-patrol mission: don't leave any clues behind to show you've been there; be as invisible as possible.

I filled in my scrape before working my way carefully from the airfield on knees and elbows. My clothes were soaking wet. They were going to stay soaking wet in this cold night air until we got back on board HMS *Antrim*.

Me, Mack and Jake joined up with 15 Troop to retrace our steps over the boggy terrain to our RV at the northern end of Pebble Island. We now had as much information as we could get in the time we'd been on the island. The next thing was to put it together, and work out our plan of attack.

Chapter 4
PLAN OF ATTACK

Back on board the Antrim we sorted through all the information. I was very impressed with the material from Banco and the rest of 15 Troop. They'd numbered every house from one to ten and made a list of everyone who entered or left them, or anyone they could see through the windows with their binoculars. With descriptions like *Short bald man round about fifty with dark moustache*, *Young woman about twenty wearing red anorak* and *Man in pilot's uniform*, it was easy to decide which houses were occupied by civilians and which ones by the Argentinians.

15 Troop had also made a close inspection of the Wool Shed and counted over 100 men stationed in it. With the 60 enemy soldiers and mechanics estimated to be at the airfield, plus the officers and

pilots, there were about 200 enemy personnel on Pebble Island. Supported by a dozen well-armed aircraft, they were no walk-over.

The whole of our unit assembled in the *Antrim*'s wardroom for a briefing. As before, the map of the Falkland Islands was on the wall, along with a much larger and more detailed one of Pebble Island.

'Right,' said Captain Wilson. 'Thanks to the OP by Troops 14 and 15 we've got a good idea of what we're up against: two hundred Argentinians and twelve aircraft. And there are fifteen of us.

'Normally I'd say that was pretty good odds. No problems nipping in, blowing up the aircraft and pulling out. But, and it's a big but: there are civilians to be taken into consideration. According to 15 Troop there are twenty of them, including five children and two elderly people. The danger is that if we run into stiff opposition and have to get help from the *Antrim*, a stray shell could hit a civilian target. So, to ensure we won't require the *Antrim*'s support, we'll need a force larger than us. Luckily, the task force is nearly here.

'I've been in touch with it and the

estimated time of arrival for HMS *Zeus,* which is carrying G Squadron SAS, is tomorrow afternoon. I've arranged that our squadron will transfer to the *Zeus* once it comes within range. We'll do it by chopper as soon as darkness falls, to avoid the prying eyes of the enemy knowing what we're up to.

'The reason for joining G Squadron, rather than them transferring to the *Antrim*, is because the *Zeus* carries four Sea Kings as well as Harrier jump jets. So, we'll be able to have a mass assault on Pebble Island using three of the choppers.

'We'll spend some time on the *Zeus*, bringing G Squadron up to date and finalizing plans for the operation.'

'We do the work, and I bet G Squadron grab all the glory,' muttered Jake.

'What glory?' grinned Mack. 'This is a secret mission –'

'When you two have finished arguing, do you mind if I continue?' cut in Captain Wilson.

Mack gave an apologetic grin, and Captain Wilson carried on.

'The first thing we have to do on the island is to get the civilians out of the way, to a safe distance from the airfield, where most of the action is going to be. 15 Troop know the settlement, so they will be responsible for this, helped by 16 Troop. It won't be easy; some of the civilians may be reluctant to leave their home. You're to try persuasion first. If that doesn't succeed, tell them that the island is going to be bombed and that they could well be killed. If that doesn't work: kidnap them. The important thing is to get them out of harm's way – and without the enemy realizing what's going on.

'At the same time as 15 and 16 are dealing with the civilians, 14 Troop and my own troop, 13, will get on to the airfield and place explosives on all the aircraft, for detonation by remote control. We'll do this in three teams of two, with the seventh man acting as look-out while the explosives are being attached. Andy and Zed will deal with four of the Pucaras. Myself and Tony will take care of another three and the Alouette. Jerry and Mack from 14 Troop will deal with the remaining Pucara and the three Mi-24s. Jake will be the look-out.'

Jake gave a sigh of deep gloom. 'Look-out,' he groaned. 'Kept out of the action.'

Captain Wilson added, 'The men from G Squadron will act as cover for the operation: some of them at the Wool Shed, some round the airfield and the remainder covering the houses occupied by the enemy.'

Regardless of Jake's gloomy opinion, Mack and I exchanged looks and grinned happily. Thank heavens we were going to be part of the attack force! I hadn't fancied nurse-maiding the civilians, nor lying in hiding, watching the enemy in case they got suspicious. Give me action every time!

'Needless to say, the whole operation will have to be carried out very quickly,' continued Captain Wilson. 'Surprise is one of our greatest weapons.'

'What do we do with the civilians after we've blown up the aircraft?' asked Marty Nielsen from 16 Troop.

'Keep them away from the action,' said Wilson. 'Once we're sure the aircraft have been destroyed, *Antrim* and *Zeus* will start to bombard the airfield. Hopefully, this will persuade the Argentinians to surrender. With their aircraft gone, there's no way they can retaliate effectively. Once they've surrendered, we can send a force ashore to take them prisoner and to establish our own base on Pebble Island. The civilians can then return to their homes.

'After that, they should be safe. It's unlikely the Argentinians will launch an air attack on Pebble Island, especially with a large number of their own men held prisoner on it.'

'Say the Argentinians don't surrender,' asked Zed. 'Are the *Antrim* and *Zeus* going to shell their positions until they do?'

Wilson smiled.

'And possibly destroy the houses and the Wool Shed in the process? I don't think that will go down well with the civilians. No, if the Argentinians don't surrender straight away, it'll be our job to make sure they do.'

As we filed out of the briefing-room, Jake let out another one of his groans.

'Thirty-one of us against two hundred, and we're going to force them to surrender?' he queried. 'Why is it we never get the odds in our favour?'

'Because we're the SAS!' grinned Mack. 'Go on, admit it, Jake, you'd hate it if the odds were the other way round. It'd be boring, wouldn't it?'

Chapter 5
TRAGEDY

That night it was good to sleep somewhere warm and dry. The whole of the previous night had been spent stretched out in a cold, wet scrape. The next morning we were up with the dawn and listening to the latest reports on the progress of the task force.

The problem with any convoy is that it has to travel at the speed of the slowest ship. In the case of the task force, although some of the destroyers and frigates could make 25 knots, the tankers which carried the all-important fuel could only travel at 15 knots, so that was its speed. This meant that the journey from Britain to the Falkland Islands had already taken three weeks. That had given the enemy more time to strengthen its bases on the islands.

British ships already in the Atlantic when the Argentinians had invaded the Falklands had been ordered to Ascension Island to await the task force. The navy's top brass had decided that it was too dangerous to send vessels on their own to the Falklands.

While we waited for the *Zeus* to arrive, we kept fit and practised preparing the explosives and sticking them to various parts of the ship. This worried the *Antrim*'s crew, until we pointed out that we were using dummy detonators. Some of them seemed reassured, though not all of them! We didn't like to tell them that there had been accidents with the plastic explosive we were using, even without detonators.

We spent as much time as we could on deck, getting fresh air, even though it was bitterly cold. Down below, there was always a smell of diesel. Give me fresh air any time, even if it is freezing.

Once we saw two Argentinian planes flying towards us. I held my breath as they came nearer and nearer, waiting for them to attack. If they did, there was very little I could do. At the last moment, the planes turned away, obviously deciding to keep their distance from the *Antrim*'s guns. They were probably only on a recce mission.

Finally, we heard that the lead ships of the task force were approaching. I spent the next hour scanning the horizon through my binoculars, watching for them, eager for the *Zeus* to arrive so that we could get on with our mission. At last, I saw the *Zeus*, bristling with guns and aircraft, ploughing through the heaving sea towards us. A great cheer went up from everyone on the *Antrim*'s deck.

'Now we can get some action!!' said Mack delightedly.

'What do you think we've been doing so far?' complained Jake. 'We took back South Georgia, remember?'

'Yeah, but that was small fry compared with what we're going to do,' said Mack. 'Now we've got the whole crowd, we can really sort these Argentinians out!'

With darkness falling, our squadron assembled near the helipad, prepared for the transfer to the *Zeus*. The wind had picked up to gale force and the sea was extremely rough, tossing the *Antrim* and the *Zeus* about as if they were toy boats.

'We'll cross in two trips because of these conditions,' Captain Wilson informed us. 'Troops 14 and 15 will go over first, then the chopper will come back for the rest of us. Right, men, load up. Let's go.'

Me, Mack, Jake, Banco, Dobbs, Frog and Mick clambered on board the Sea King with all our gear.

The Sea King comes in several varieties, from the small four-seater attack type to the large assault ones, with some other sorts in between. Ours was a Mark 4, which is an assault transport gunship made to carry twenty-seven men. So, in theory, the whole of our squadron could have fitted inside it. Indeed, in an emergency, we would all have piled in. Although it was only a five-minute journey, the atrocious weather had made Captain Wilson decide to play it safe, especially as we would also be taking a lot of heavy equipment with us.

It was such a bumpy ride, with the chopper going all over the place, that I was relieved to land on the *Zeus*. The seven of us scrambled out of the chopper, hauling our bergens (backpacks) and equipment with us. Then the Sea King took off for the *Antrim* and the next load.

Some familiar faces from G Squadron had gathered to welcome us. One of the first I saw was Lobby Lewis, an old mate of mine whom I'd been on many operations with.

'So you're still alive then, Jerry!' grinned Lobby. 'The Argentinians haven't blown you up yet?'

'No chance!' I grinned back. 'And we've made sure there are enough of them around to give you lot something to do. You've had it easy on your cruise from England!'

'Cruise?!' laughed Lobby. 'You should see how cramped the *Zeus* is below decks. I've been more comfortable in a jail.'

'Here come the rest of our mob,' said Frog.

The *whump whump whump* of the Sea King's main rotor blades pierced the noise of the howling wind and the crashing waves. The wind-blown spray made it difficult to see its lights, but the chopper was there. Then, suddenly, the *whump whump whump* died away and the lights disappeared . . .

Dobbs looked at me, stunned.

'*It's gone down!*' he yelled. '*The chopper's gone down!*'

Chapter 6
RE-FORMING

The next few moments on board the Zeus were frantic. Powerful searchlights began scanning the sea in the direction of the Antrim. But the huge waves and thick spray made it difficult to see anything. One thing was certain: there was no sign of the downed chopper. I felt sick. It's bad enough losing a mate or two, but a whole pack of them . . .

Boats were being lowered from the *Zeus*. I wanted to get in one of them and join the search – those were my mates out there. But the sailors wouldn't let me. They knew what they were doing and I didn't, so I glumly left them to it.

Now, one of the *Zeus*'s own helicopters took off and began combing the area between us and the *Antrim*, going backwards and forwards, hovering as low and as slow as possible, shining its lights down on the heaving sea. I saw a head bob among the waves, then disappear.

'*There!*' I shouted, pointing. '*Over there!*'

But my voice was lost in the noise of the helicopter, the howling wind and the sound of the waves crashing against the side of the ship.

Most people were now lined up on deck, holding on to the rail as the *Zeus* rolled and lurched, desperate to see if we could spot anyone or signs of debris from the helicopter, in the hope that our mates had found something to cling on to in that terrible sea.

I saw that one of the rescue boats had found someone and was hauling him out of the water.

Then the helicopter halted in a hover and trained a light on another figure in the sea. Who it was? We couldn't tell, because it was too far away. A rescue boat was already heading there. Soon someone else was dragged out.

Two survivors so far. Where were the rest?

We stayed by the rail and watched helplessly as the search went on for over two hours, even though we all knew that after half an hour people were wasting their time. No one could survive in those conditions for long. Minutes, maybe. Tens of minutes, no.

We learned that the rescued men were Pete Hudson from 16 Troop and Zed Zanu from 13 Troop. All the rest of our mates had died. Nearly half of our squadron dead in the space of a few seconds – Andy Swann, Tony Weathers, Wiggy Jones, Nick Randall, Marty Nielsen, Captain Wilson. Not forgetting the pilots of the Sea King.

I don't think any of us slept that night. In a way, we still kept hoping that some kind of miracle would happen and that Captain Wilson would lead the others through the door, having clambered up out of the sea. All of us had been in tough spots before, where we thought it was the end, and we'd managed to cheat death. But this time there was no cheating death for any of them. They were gone.

We met up with Zed and Pete after they'd been checked over by the medicos. Neither was exactly sure what had gone wrong.

'I don't know whether it was mechanical failure, the bad weather or pilot error,' said

Pete. 'One minute we were bumping along OK, the next the chopper nose-dived, as though a huge hand had lifted it up by the tail rotor.'

'I blame the wind,' said Zed. 'It was getting stronger every minute.'

'The chopper went all over the place,' Pete continued. 'Zed and I were slung out through the main door, nearly getting chopped in half by the main rotor blades when it turned on its side before hitting the water.'

'The pilot shouldn't have left the *Antrim*. Conditions were too bad for flying,' said Pete.

Zed shook his head.

'Don't blame him,' he said. 'He was just carrying out orders.'

We never found out what caused the accident. All we did know for certain was that we had lost a load of our mates.

The next morning there was an awkward atmosphere in the briefing-room on the *Zeus*. We held a minute's silence for our lost comrades before getting down to business. Men die, but war goes on.

Brigadier Sholto had come with G

Squadron on the *Zeus*, and he took over as company commander. The first thing he did was to re-form us to bring the units up to strength. Zed and Pete joined me, Mack and Jake in 14 Troop. For the moment it meant that we'd have one man more than usual, but as we'd been one man short so far, since Rob had got wounded, I reckoned that balanced it out.

Next we began sorting out who would be doing what on the assault on the airfield on Pebble Island.

The five of us in 14 Troop from D Squadron, plus two of the blokes from G Squadron's 6 Troop, would carry out the attack on the aircraft.

16 Troop, who were already detailed to nurse-maid the civilians, would still do that, but would be working now with 7 Troop from G Squadron.

The other two men from 6 Troop, along with Troops 8 and 9 from G Squadron, would act as the main back-up force, stationed round the airfield. In addition, thirty-five Commandos would be joining us. They'd be split between the Wool Shed and the settlement, ready to act as support if needed.

The order of the demolition teams was now changed. Mack and I were still assigned to take out the three Mi-24s and one of the Pucaras. Zed and Pete would take out four of the Pucaras. The two guys from 6 Troop, Jazzer and Ruff, would deal with the remaining three Pucaras and the Alouette. Jake would still be acting as look-out for all of us while we were doing this.

The plan was now set. So was the time. We'd be going in when we hoped the enemy least expected us: 02.00 hours.

Chapter 7
ATTACK!

I have to admit it felt weird as I climbed into the Sea King helicopter that night with the rest of the guys for our trip to Pebble Island. A part of me couldn't help but think of the last Sea King trip – the quick five-minute hop between the *Antrim* and the *Zeus*. This one to Pebble Island was going to take three times as long. And conditions were nearly as bad as the previous night.

As we lifted off from the *Zeus* I looked down at the raging sea just below us and thought about Wiggy and Marty and Captain Wilson and all the rest of the boys who'd gone down beneath those ugly great waves.

We were all silent during the flight. I expect we were waiting for something to go wrong, but we just gritted our teeth and got on with it. Some men die, some live. In a war situation, you just hope you're one of those who lives.

This time there were twenty of us in each of the three choppers heading to Pebble Island. Faces blackened. Body armour. Fully kitted up and armed. As well as our M16 rifles, ammo and grenades, me, Jake and Mack were carrying the explosives for our mission. We were going to be using PE4 plastic explosives. It looks and feels like white Plasticine, and you can push it into any shape you want. And it sticks to different sorts of surface. On its own it's *usually* safe . . . though I stress the 'usually'. Accidents can always happen. It's when a detonator is pushed into it and primed, ready to blow, that PE4 becomes dangerous.

We'd be using remote-control detonators in the PE4, so we could set off all the explosions at the same time. The last thing we wanted was one of the aircraft going up while the rest of us were still wiring up the others.

Me and the rest of 14 Troop were in the first Sea King, along with G Squadron. G Squadron had the heavy weaponry in case it came to a fire-fight, including the Brunswick RAW grenade-launchers which, when added to the MI6, made them formidable weapons. They were also packing enough ammunition to give us each 400 rounds for our machine guns, as well as ammo for their own rifles. Also on board were extra grenades and bombs for the 81-mm mortar.

Strong winds hit us as we flew, spray from the sea coming through the open door as our pilot kept as low as he could over the sea to escape radar detection. The other two choppers flew alongside us through the night sky.

The fifteen-minute flight over the vicious sea seemed to take forever, but finally we reached Pebble Island. This time the choppers landed us further south than before, but we were still two hours' march from the Argentinian airfield. As soon as we troopers had hit the boggy, moss-covered ground, the three choppers took off on their way back to the *Zeus*.

We made good time over the slippery, rocky ground, reaching the perimeter of the airfield just after 04.00 hours. As before, the airfield was in darkness, although some light was filtering through a chink in a black-out curtain. The settlement near by was also in darkness.

There was no time for any last-minute double-checks on what we were supposed to do. We'd rehearsed the operation time and time again on the ship. Every man knew what to do. We'd talked through the theory, now came the reality.

Banco, Dobbs and the rest of 15 Troop headed for the settlement, along with the rest of 6 Troop and 8 and 9 Troop. The Commandos made their way towards the Wool Shed. Meanwhile me, Mack, Jake, Pete and Zed, along with Jazzer and Ruff from 6 Troop, aimed for the aircraft.

On the recce we noticed that the Argentinians only patrolled the airfield's perimeter fence about every hour. Whether this was because of laziness or because they didn't fancy being out in the freezing cold night air, I didn't know. All I did know was that it made our job of getting over the short fence much easier.

Once we were inside the perimeter fence, I checked the airfield through my night-glasses. As before, the aircraft were spread out. Six of the Pucaras were at the far side of the airfield from our position; two of the Mi-24s and a Pucara were nearer to us; and the rest – the Alouette helicopter, the other Mi-24 and the remaining Pucara – were scattered in the middle.

'Guards!' hissed Mack next to me, pointing to the Pucara alongside the two Mi-24s.

I trained my night-glasses on it. Sure enough, there were two soldiers, both carrying rifles, crouched beneath the plane. I guessed they were sheltering there from the cold, which was why we hadn't spotted them immediately.

'OK,' I whispered back.

I turned to the others and indicated the Pucara with the two guards under it.

'Mack and I will take it and the two men. We'll also take the two Mi-24s next to it. When we've finished with them, we'll join Jazzer and Ruff to take care of the last Mi-24. OK?'

The others nodded.

'Let's go,' muttered Pete.

Mack and I headed towards the Pucara with the two Argentinians, bent double and zigzagging, stopping every now and then to take stock, desperate not to make any noise.

My hope was that the two guards would have their Arctic gear on, with thick hat flaps covering their ears, but you could never be sure. Some men on guard duty are so lax that you could drive a truck past them and they wouldn't notice. Others are so nervous that even a mouse farting would make them jump and start firing.

We made it to the Pucara, sneaking up behind the two Argentinian guards. Now I could hear them muttering to each other. But Mack and I crept even nearer until we were right behind them.

'*Por favor,*' I whispered in my basic Spanish.

The guard nearest to me turned. When he saw my rifle pointing straight at him, right between his eyes, he nearly fainted. Mack had his rifle trained on the second guard.

'Open your mouths and you're dead,' I told them in broken Spanish. 'Put your hands up.'

As I'd said before, I only had a rough command of Spanish, but it was enough to get the message across to these guys. Immediately their hands shot up. They looked terrified. They deserved to be. In their position, suddenly to come face to face with two heavily armed men with blackened faces would have terrified me as well.

We tied their hands and feet together and gagged them. Next we started on the aircraft.

We did the Pucara first.

The Pucara is a tall plane, so I had to give Mack a leg up on to a wing. While he began setting the PE4 and the detonators there and in the cockpit, I hurried over to the nearest Mi-24 to wire it up.

The hatch of the chopper's hold was open, so I climbed in and fixed some plastic to the roof, pushing a detonator into it. When it went off it would bring the main rotor crashing down. All the while I kept my ears open for any noise to indicate the enemy's approach. No matter how many times you do this sort of thing, there is always tension, a feeling like butterflies in your stomach while you wait for the enemy to find you.

From the hold, I clambered into the chopper's cockpit and stuck wads of plastic on the controls, again pushing detonators into them.

Then I jumped down to the ground and saw that Mack had already finished wiring up his PE4 on the Pucara and was now dealing with the other Mi-24.

I gestured towards Jazzer and Ruff at work on their targets, to indicate that I was going over to join them to take care of the last Mi-24. Mack nodded.

When I got to Jazzer and Ruff, they were climbing down from the Alouette.

'All done,' Ruff grinned at me. 'Including yours. Since you were taking out the guards, we thought it was only fair we did your Mi-24 for you.'

'We're going to need help moving the two guards,' I said. 'We can't leave them where they are; they'll be blown to bits when the PE4 goes off.'

Jazzer and Ruff nodded and hurried back with me to where Mack was waiting by the two bound and gagged Argentinians.

'The removal men have arrived!' joked Jazzer.

Mack and I picked up one of the prisoners, while Jazzer and Ruff took the other one.

We headed for the perimeter fence,

weighed down by the two prisoners. Soon we were joined by Pete and Zed.

'All sorted,' whispered Pete.

As we neared the fence, Jake materialized out of the darkness.

'All clear,' he muttered. 'No sign of any enemy activity.'

'Any action from the houses?' I asked.

'Not that I could hear,' said Jake. 'Nor from the Wool Shed. So, fingers crossed, our blokes have done what they're supposed to.'

'It looks like it's all going to plan,' said Mack.

And that's when the shooting started.

Chapter 8
RESCUE

We heard the *rat-a-tat-tat* of an automatic rifle, followed by more gunfire.

'Sounds like it's coming from the Wool Shed,' said Zed.

'Could be from one of the houses,' said Jake.

Lights were already appearing on the airfield as the Argentinians roused themselves. We didn't wait. We grabbed our two prisoners, hauled them over the fence and dumped them on the ground on the other side. Then we set off the remote-control detonators.

The aircraft blowing up was an incredible display of explosive power. All twelve of them – the Pucaras, the three Mi-24s and the little Alouette – erupted into massive balls of flame, lighting up the darkness. It was an amazing sight, as if everything in front of us had just been blown apart. We ducked as bits of burning aircraft flew through the air over us.

'How much PE4 did you use, for heaven's sake?' I demanded of Jazzer and Ruff.

Jazzer grinned.

'Remember the SAS rule: add P for Plenty!' he chuckled.

'Yes, but not enough to blow your mates up as well!' I said.

The explosions had caused consternation on the airfield. Through my night-glasses I watched as tent flaps burst open and dozy, half-dressed Argentinians fled from the smouldering bits raining down on them, disbelief on their faces as they stared at the destruction all around them.

Some began firing wildly into the night. We let them have return fire, with the guys from 8 Troop, who were acting as our back-up, joining in. The amount of fire-power unnerved the Argentinians, who scuttled behind any available bit of shelter.

With all this going on, it was difficult to hear if there was still firing from the Wool Shed, about a kilometre away.

'Can you hold them?' I shouted at Jake. 'Me and Mack'll go and see what's going on at the shed, in case our lads have run into trouble.'

'No problem,' said Jake. 'We'll keep them pinned down easy from here while they wonder about what's hit them.'

With that, Jake let off a burst to keep enemy heads down. Meanwhile, the aircraft burned away, smoke and sparks billowing up into the sky. The air was filled with the acrid smell of burning plastic, rubber and metal.

Mack and I ran off to the Wool Shed, zigzagging at a crouch, just in case the Argentinians were now alert enough to spot us. We ran into Banco Watts urging an elderly couple along a rough track, yelling at them to keep their heads down.

'What's happening?' I asked him. 'Who's doing the shooting?'

'Not us,' replied Banco. 'We got all the civilians out nice and easy. Well, most of them nice and easy. One couple didn't want to go, so Frog and Dobbs had to "encourage" them, shall we say! They said they're going to lodge a complaint with the CO.'

'What about the officers and pilots who were in the houses?' asked Mack.

'All taken prisoner,' said Banco.

We could hear the gunfire clearer now. It was definitely coming from near the Wool Shed. The Commandos must have run into some resistance.

'We're going over there to see what's up,' I told Banco.

'Me and Frog will come with you,' said Banco. 'Dobbs and Mick and the others can handle this lot now.' With that, Banco shouted, 'Dobbs!'

Dobbs appeared, shepherding a young couple to safety.

'What?' he asked.

'Look after these two,' Banco said. 'I'm going to grab Frog and go with Jerry and Mack to sort out the Wool Shed. OK?'

Dobbs nodded.

'You got it,' he said.

The three of us hurried away. We saw Frog, and Banco shouted at him to join us. Then we headed for the Wool Shed and the sound of gunfire.

Through the darkness we could see the huge shape of the Wool Shed towering over the houses near it. Gunfire was coming down at it from a hill about a kilometre away. The fire was being returned from inside the shed. We hesitated, wondering who was where: were the Commandos up on the hill or in the Wool Shed? We got our answer when rifle fire from the hill started coming in our direction, bullets slamming and tearing into the boggy ground near our feet.

Me, Mack, Banco and Frog dived behind the scanty cover that the nearby rocks and mossy banks provided. Working our way forwards on our bellies, we joined a group of about ten Commandos in the shelter of the Wool Shed, returning gunfire up the slope.

'What's happening?' asked Banco.

One of the Commandos scowled and gestured up the hill.

'We thought we had them all nicely trapped,' he said. 'We ran in here and fired off a burst into the air to wake them up and let them know we meant business. Straight away their hands went up and we thought it was all over. But about a dozen of them managed to break out through a side door which we hadn't seen.'

'Didn't you have back-up round there?' asked Mack.

'Yes,' nodded the Commando. 'We had two guys there. They Argentinians shot one and took the other hostage. They're up there on the hill with him right now. We can't use any heavy weaponry on them in case of hitting him. Plus, we can't go after them until we've made sure the ones here can't cause any trouble.'

'How are you doing that?' asked Mack.

'We've ordered them to take off their boots, socks and belts,' the Commando answered. 'They can't do much in bare feet with their trousers round their ankles! Trouble is, it's taking time to collect all the belts, boots and socks.'

'OK,' I said. 'We'll go up the hill and sort them out. What's the name of the guy they've got?'

'Paul Anders,' answered the Commando.

'Right. We need a diversion while we get up there. If you and your mates keep them busy, we'll go round the back of them.' Turning to Banco and Frog, I said, 'You two go round to the left, me and Mack will take the right. OK?'

Banco nodded.

'No worries,' he said.

Banco and Frog disappeared into the darkness towards the left side of the hill. Mack and I wormed our way on our bellies to the right. The Commandos started firing at the Argentinians on the hill, shooting deliberately high so that they wouldn't hit Paul. Mack and I began to climb up the back of the hill.

The higher and nearer we got to the Argentinians' position, the more dangerous it became. Not only were we worried about being seen by the enemy, but some of the Commandos in the Wool Shed were shooting low.

'Someone ought to teach those blokes how to shoot properly,' grumbled Mack.

'They're shooting to miss,' I reminded him.

'Yes, but I want them to shoot to miss *me*,' said Mack as a bullet from the Wool Shed ricocheted dangerously off a rock near him.

We crawled up the hill until we were just above the Argentinians' position. With my night-glasses I could make out six of them bunched together behind a low ridge of rock, firing at the Commandos in the Wool Shed. The rest of them were crouched behind their comrades, holding down Paul Anders.

'It's going to be difficult to shoot into them without hitting our own man,' muttered Mack. 'They're so tightly bunched together.'

'In that case, why don't we drop a flash-bang in the middle of them?' I suggested.

The flash-bang is a stun-grenade that is filled with an explosive mixture of mercury and magnesium. When it goes off it disorientates the enemy for about forty-five seconds. Sometimes longer. It's best used in enclosed situations, like when you're trying to free a hostage from an armed terrorist inside a plane or a building. But even here it would have an effect. Also, because we'd be using it outside, the air would help weaken the effects of the CS gas in it. In a confined space, you need to wear a respirator to deal with the fumes. I always keep a flash-bang with me as part of my basic equipment. You never know when it will come in handy.

'It's worth a try,' said Mack. 'Do you think you can drop it accurately from here?'

I looked at the distance I'd have to lob it. It was a long way. Still, it was our best bet; there was nothing else we could try.

'I'll give it a go,' I said. 'Just keep your fingers crossed that Banco and Frog haven't decided to do some hand-to-combat, otherwise they're going to get a face-full of magnesium flare as well.'

With that, I pulled out the flash-bang, triggered it and let fly.

Mack and I ducked down, turning our faces away from the Argentinians. There was a very loud *BANG!!* and a bright, white flash.

Mack and I stood up and turned round. The flash-bang had done its work. From the enemy position there came yells and screams, mostly from fear and disorientation. When a flash-bang goes off, everything goes white: you can't see; you can't hear; you can't even think.

Mack and I made it to the Argentinians just as some of them were starting to recover. We didn't give them the chance. Most of them had dropped their guns so that they could cover their ears and eyes when the flash-bang went off. We kicked their guns away from them and shoved the barrels of our rifles at them to let them know we meant business.

There was a scrabbling noise from behind us, and Frog and Banco arrived.

'You might have let us known you were

going to pull a stunt like that,' complained Banco. 'We could have been hit by it.'

'But you weren't,' I said.

'That's not the point,' insisted Banco. 'The last time I was caught up with a flash-bang I couldn't hear anything for two days.'

'The point is we've saved our man, even if he is a little bit the worse for wear. And none of us got injured,' said Mack.

'I still think you should have let us know what you were going to do,' grumbled Banco.

'I will next time,' I said. 'I promise.'

Mack and I shepherded the still-dazed Argentinians back down the hillside, while Banco and Frog checked on the Commando, Paul Anders. He was bruised and cut about the face where the Argentinians had hit him as they forced him to go with them, and still a bit shell-shocked from the effect of my flash-bang, but otherwise he was OK.

Now it was just a case of mopping up.

Chapter 9
THE BIG ASSAULT

Six hours later it was all over. Reinforcements of Marines had landed from the *Zeus* and taken charge of the prisoners. They began to turn the Argentinian camp at the airfield and the Wool Shed into makeshift prisoner-holding points. With a large number of their own men being kept prisoner on Pebble Island, the Argentinians would be unlikely to start shelling it.

The civilians returned to their homes. Most of them were grateful to be back under British control, although one couple complained bitterly about being woken up in the middle of the night and made to hang around in the cold.

'I need my regular sleep,' the husband, a Mr Patch, moaned to me as I walked with him back to his home. 'I could get ill if I don't have a proper sleep.'

'But say we'd left you in bed and the fighting had got worse and shells had started dropping on your house?' I pointed out.

'I'm insured,' said Mr Patch. 'The insurance company would have paid for it.'

Everyone else was delighted, and people insisted we have a cup of tea with them before returning to the *Zeus*. Then someone suggested breakfast . . . Soon I was tucking in to one of the best meals I've ever had in my life: fried eggs, bacon, sausages, toast and marmalade, along with big mugs of sweet tea. I made a mental note to try and get the food replaced from our own stores. After all, supplies were probably hard to get in this out-of-the-way spot, and we didn't want to take everything the islanders had.

As soon as the island was declared secure, with the Argentinian prisoners in safe hands, we were helicoptered back to the *Zeus*, leaving the Commandos and Marines on Pebble Island to tidy up. We felt great – our bellies were full, the objective had been achieved and, best of all, we hadn't lost any of our men. Mission accomplished!

* * *

Back on board the *Zeus* we grabbed ourselves six hours' solid sleep. When we woke up and went on deck, a grey sleet was falling, obscuring our view of Pebble Island in the distance.

'What a terrible place this is,' moaned Jake. 'Cold winds and rain. Why can't we get an assignment in the desert again? I miss the sand and hot sunshine.'

I grinned at this. Whichever part of the world we were in, Jake moaned about it. Here, he complained about the wind and rain. When we were in the Arctic, it had been the freezing temperatures. In the jungle, it was the humidity and the insects. The year before we'd been out in the Gulf, carrying out a covert operation. Then, Jake had had as much sand and sunshine as anyone could handle in a lifetime, and he'd moaned about it: it was too hot, the landscape was all the same, just boring sand and rocks, There was no pleasing Jake!

We spent the first part of the morning sorting through our equipment, checking it out and making any repairs that were needed.

After any engagement it's always wise to

make sure that every moving part in a gun works. Unless you do, you could end up with a gun that jams just when need it most.

Also, after an engagement, it's time for getting out the sewing kit and repairing any holes in your clothing caused by things like bullets and barbed wire. Look after your equipment and it will look after you. And that means every bit of equipment down to the smallest item.

Just after lunch the call came: Brigadier Sholto wanted all SAS men assembled in the mess hall, which was doubling as our briefing-room.

'Debriefing about Pebble Island?' suggested Jazzer.

'Unlikely,' said Banco. 'I bet the Brig knows it all already. No, my betting is it'll be details of our next mission.'

Banco was right.

Brigadier Sholto was standing by the familiar large map of the Falklands when we walked into the mess hall. He waited until we'd all taken our seats.

'Right, men,' he began, 'now the task force is finally here, we are ready to retake the Falkland Islands.'

'Nothing small, then,' muttered Jake next to me in his usual gloomy fashion.

'The planned time for our main assault is dawn on twenty-seventh May, in four days' time,' the Brigadier continued. 'The attack will be in three prongs. About five thousand British troops will be going ashore by landing-craft to establish the beach-head at San Carlos Water, which is seventy kilometres west of the capital, Port Stanley. At the same time, a further five thousand will be making a beach assault in the south of East Falkland, at Goose Green. They will push eastwards to Port Stanley.

'The third prong of the attack will be coming from the south-east, with one thousand Marine Commandos landing at Bluff Cove to cut off any retreating Argentinian forces and stop them reaching Port Stanley.'

The Brigadier used his stick to point out the three locations on the map.

'All three assaults will be supported by heavy gunfire on the enemy positions from the ships offshore, as well as assault troops being landed by Sea King helicopters, but the ships and all the assault troops will be vulnerable to attack. However, there is a problem with this plan –'

'The enemy?' quipped Mack, and all of us laughed. Even the Brigadier gave a smile.

'In fact, Mack, although you thought you were joking, you've hit the nail on the head,' he said.

'Mack the military genius!' cracked Jazzer, and again there was laughter in the room, which quietened down as the Brigadier waved his hand to get our attention.

'The truth is the Argentinians have had a lot of time to dig themselves in. If this major assault is to succeed, then it's up to us to do two things.

'One, we have to reduce the effectiveness of the enemy's defences. In other words, we do the same as we did on Pebble Island: knock out as many of their planes as we can. The fewer aircraft the Argentinians can get into the air, the less chance they have of attacking our guys when they land on the beaches.

'Two, capture suitable sites so that our own assault helicopters can land and bring in more troops. Most of the flat areas on tops of hills are being used by the enemy

73

as helipads. It's your job to make as many of them as possible safe for our own choppers.'

We all nodded. The Brigadier was right. A full frontal attack against an enemy who'd dug in usually meant heavy casualties, and too often led to a major defeat. Working behind enemy lines, preparing the way for a major assault, was what we in the SAS did best. It was dangerous work, but that's why we'd all volunteered for it.

'You'll be going in as soon as darkness falls tonight,' the Brigadier continued. '14 and 15 Troop, you'll be preparing the way for the assault at San Carlos. 6 and 7 Troop will be doing the same for Goose Green, and 8 and 9 Troop will be handling the area around Bluff Cove.

'One word of warning: it's quite likely that, as a result of the successful raid on Pebble Island, the Argentinians here will have beefed up security, planting booby-traps round their airfields and other potential targets. So, be prepared for anything.

'Also, because we expect East Falkland to be better defended, with more up-to-date defensive and electronic search equipment than on Pebble Island, you'll be going in by sea. We don't want to alert the enemy by having them spot a whole group of Sea Kings coming at them. So, it'll be small boats and paddles. No motors. Nothing to warn the enemy that you're landing.'

'Paddles!' groaned Jake next to me. 'I'll be worn out before we reach the shore.'

'One last thing,' said the Brigadier. 'Try to keep radio silence, just in case the enemy picks up your transmissions. This is a secret assault. Be invisible, and hit them hard. It's up to you to make sure the Argentinian defences are in a bad way when our main assault is launched. The better you do, the more of our men will survive.'

Chapter 10
CLOSE TO THE ENEMY

The *Zeus* was thirty kilometres offshore when a launch was lowered into the heaving sea and me, Mack, Zed, Pete, Banco, Dobbs, Frog and Mick clambered down into it, bringing the equipment we reckoned we'd need. Apart from two inflatable boats and paddles, our bergens and rations, we were also taking some useful weaponry. As well as our regular rifles and pistols, we loaded grenade-launchers, rocket-launchers and missiles. If we were going to make a big dent in the Argentinian defences, we needed some heavy-duty weapons.

The trip to East Falkland was bumpy and wet, the launch being bounced up and down by the waves and us getting soaked with salty seawater.

'If this is what this part of the journey's

like, I don't fancy the paddling bit,' grumbled Jake.

'Don't worry,' said Mick. 'We're being dropped near the shore, where the sea won't be so rough. And we'll only have about three kilometres to paddle. It'll be a piece of cake.'

As it turned out, Mick, the optimist, was wrong and Jake, the grumbler, was right. The launch slowed down off San Carlos, and we loaded the heavy equipment into one of the inflatables with Banco, Dobbs, Mick and Frog, while the rest of us – me, Mack, Jake, Pete and Zed – got into the other one.

The journey to the shore was a nightmare. The surging sea threw our inflatable about as if we were just a cork bobbing about on it. On the positive side, the rough weather made it difficult for us to be spotted. We were also lucky that it was an incoming tide, so it pushed us towards the shore. If we'd been battling against an outgoing one, we'd probably have ended up in the middle of the South Atlantic.

As we got near land, the sea calmed down and we headed to an inlet.

Things were still tricky, and we needed all our strength to keep the boat from being flipped over by some high waves. Finally we made it to the shore, the waves pushing our inflatable up on to a stony beach. The other boat arrived shortly after us.

'See?' snorted Jake sarcastically to Mick. 'Piece of cake indeed!'

'I've been in rougher seas than that,' responded Mick. 'Did I ever tell you about the time I got caught in a whirlpool off the African coast?'

'No, but I'm sure you will,' said Jake.

We hauled the two inflatables up the beach on to the marshy ground behind it. Then Pete and Zed went off to scout along the shore towards the east, while Banco and Dobbs went westwards. They were looking for somewhere to make camp. Banco and Dobbs were back first, after half an hour.

'We've found a spot,' Banco announced. 'There's a large crack in the rock-face which goes into a cave. It's a bit of a squeeze to get in, which means there's less chance of the opening being spotted – especially if we hang a camouflage net over it.'

'Can we fit the inflatables in as they are, without letting the air out?' Jake asked.

'Just about,' nodded Dobbs. 'It's worth a try.'

'Good,' said Jake. 'I hate inflating these things.'

Ten minutes later, Pete and Zed rejoined us, looking fed up.

'Nothing,' said Pete. 'It's flat as a pancake in that direction. No trees. Nothing.'

'No problem, Banco and Dobbs have found our new home for us,' said Mack. 'Right, lads, let's get indoors and make ourselves comfortable.'

We carried the inflatables and all our equipment the kilometre or so to the cave entrance found by Banco and Dobbs. As they said, getting in really was a bit of a squeeze, but once through the crack, the cave opened out into a perfectly comfortable living space. Even the boats got through.

We stashed them at the back of the cave, along with the heavy weaponry and ammo. Then we settled down to grab some sleep, taking it in turns to do guard duty.

* * *

As dawn came up, we ate some rations before splitting into four two-man recce teams, with one man left to keep guard over our basecamp. We drew straws to see who was going to have that boring job. Unlucky Jake drew the short straw.

'Typical!' he groaned. 'I reckon I was born unlucky!'

As before, me and Mack paired off, while Zed and Pete, Banco and Dobbs, and Frog and Mick formed the other pairs.

Recce-ing can be a dull job, especially if you're stuck in one position for hours on end, like we had been on OP (observation patrol) checking out Pebble Island. Here, around San Carlos Water, it was going to be different. For one thing, the area we had to cover was much bigger. Also, the enemy were more scattered. We had to find out where they were, what sort of defences they had, the strength of their armour and artillery, and where the landing-sites for their air-power were.

We'd split our search area into four quadrants: north, south, east and west. Mack and I had taken the western quadrant, which bordered on the beach in San Carlos Water, the site of one of the main prongs of the planned invasion. Because we had to be mobile, we only took light equipment with us: rifle, pistol, ammo, knife and some rope. Plus water and basic rations to keep us going during the day. We also had camouflage webbing that we could roll out and slide under to dodge an air patrol. From the air, the webbing, which looks like a fishing net with leaves stuck on it, is hard to distinguish from natural landscape. We'd adapted ours to the surroundings by adding moss and rushes to it.

The first enemy site we came upon was a cluster of tents halfway up a small hill. We saw them from a distance of just over a kilometre.

We laid down flat on the boggy ground and pulled the camouflage webbing over us, and then trained our binoculars on the tents.

There were four of them, one larger than the others. Aerials poked up from this tent, and cables ran from it to a generator about fifty metres away.

I saw three men moving about, all armed with light machine-guns slung carelessly over their shoulders by the straps.

The hill itself had a large scrubby crest that looked as if it had been flattened.

'Helipad,' grunted Mack.

I nodded in agreement.

As if to confirm this, we heard the sound of a helicopter coming from the west, getting louder and louder. The main rotor's down draught blasted our position as the chopper descended to settle on the hilltop.

It was a Huey, or – to give it its full name – a Bell UH-1 Iroquois. Used a lot by the Americans in Vietnam, it was still a very reliable troop transporter.

We watched as the cabin doors opened and twelve enemy soldiers jumped to the ground, all armed and kitted out for action. They looked to me like the Argentinian Special Forces. I wondered if the Argentinians had found out that we'd landed on the island. Perhaps these were reinforcements sent to look for us. I kept my glasses trained on them as they headed down the hillside with the pilot to the large tent with aerials.

'What a pity we don't have an RPG with us,' whispered Mack.

An RPG, or rocket-propelled grenade, would have destroyed the Huey there and then. And a second one into the large tent would have taken out most of the Argentinians who'd just arrived.

'There'll be time for that later,' I hissed back. 'Today is just a recce mission, remember?'

We lay there, hidden by the camouflage webbing, watching and making notes of all movements between the tents. We were also waiting to see if the Huey would take off with the troops it had brought or leave them there. That's what a recce mission is all about: watching, then putting the pieces together to make a deduction about what's going on; finally, deciding what to do.

The men we'd first seen were much sloppier than the new arrivals, who seemed smarter and better disciplined. This is why I thought they might be Special Forces.

After observing the camp for an hour, during which nothing happened, we decided to move on.

We made a wide circle to get past the enemy tents unnoticed and headed along a small stream. The stream became narrower and narrower, until it trickled away into a bog. There was little vegetation to give us cover, apart from a few small bushes and some rushes.

We squelched through the bog for about ten kilometres. It was slow-going, taking us nearly three hours. Finally, though, it became firmer underfoot. Soon the bog was replaced by rock, with a thin coating of moss. We headed up to a ridge to check the lay of the land.

According to my calculations, from the top of the ridge we should be able to look down on the beaches of San Carlos Water where our guys were to land.

The route to the top of the ridge was exposed. Any moment I kept expecting to hear the sound of enemy choppers, but we were lucky. Mack and I made it to the top without being seen. There we lay flat and inched towards the edge to look down below.

The first thing we saw was the sea slapping against the cold greyness of the pebbly beach. The second thing was the garrison of tents. Finally, we saw that a landing-strip had been created on the rocky ground. There were trucks and armoured vehicles dotted around. Heavy artillery. And aircraft.

Riding at anchor about five kilometres offshore were four enemy ships. From the look of them, there were three destroyers and a transport ship.

We'd stumbled on the heart of the Argentinian defence. If this lot were left intact, our guys would be slaughtered when they tried to land on the beach.

Mack and I spent three hours watching the Argentinian garrison from our position on the ridge. Once again, we covered ourselves with camouflage webbing and made detailed notes in a coded shorthand, just in case they fell into enemy hands. We recorded troop movements around the camp and made a map showing the tents that looked to be the centres of activity – perhaps for communications and briefings, or accommodation for the top brass.

The landing-strip meant the Argentinians could launch fighter planes against our troops, as well as against the task-force ships. Right now there were three Dassault Mirage and two Dassault Super Etendard fighter jets parked on one side of the strip. The Etendard was basically a naval fighter plane. Did this mean that there was an Argentinian aircraft-carrier further out at sea, where there were even more of them? We knew the Etendards carried Exocet missiles, a particularly lethal piece of kit. So, two were bad news, but a carrier-load of them . . .

The ground artillery consisted mostly of anti-aircraft guns, along with three multiple rocket-launchers, all pointing out to sea.

As dusk began to fall, we decided to call it a day. We backed down the ridge to retrace our route across the bog and round the small hillside camp.

When we got to our basecamp we found that Mack and I were the last to report back. Zed and Pete had arrrived twenty minutes before us, while Banco and Dobbs and Frog and Mick had been there for over an hour. They had helped Jake get a small fire going so we could have a hot meal from our rations.

Over hot food and drink we exchanged our information.

'We found two sites where the Argentinians can land large assault choppers,' Pete reported. 'Neither of them is heavily guarded. Just a few tents and some miserable-looking men sitting outside them. The first one got a visit from a Huey, but no one got in or out of it and the chopper took off again a few minutes later, so I guess it was just a routine patrol.'

'We found a communications post,' said Frog. 'Aerials, radar, the lot. It's about ten kilometres south of here and three kilometres inland.'

'It's got heavy security round it,' added Mick. 'Looks like it's the main communications station, linking the enemy on land with their ships.'

'What about you two?' I asked Banco and Dobbs. 'Find anything?'

'Sheep,' grimaced Banco. 'Nothing but sheep.'

'Banco and I must've walked halfway across the island. No enemy positions and one derelict house,' sighed Dobbs.

'Anyone in the house?' asked Mack.

'Just sheep,' said Banco. 'I tell you, if anyone wants to know about sheep on this island, just ask me. After a day spent observing them, I'm an expert.'

Mack and I told them what we'd discovered: the small camp and the large garrison by the beach.

'Excellent!' said Jake. 'That's the place to hit.'

'And the communications base,' said Frog. 'They're bound to be linked up.'

'The garrison might be too big for us to knock out ourselves,' mused Zed. 'Why don't we call up support from the *Zeus*? Some concentrated heavy shelling from its big guns might do the trick. And the big guns of some of our other ships if it doesn't.'

'The Brigadier said to keep radio silence. Remember?' Dobbs pointed out.

'Yes,' said Zed, 'but by the time we've blown up the communications base, the enemy will know we're here, so radio silence won't be important.'

'OK,' I said. 'Let's hit the garrison last. Zed will radio the *Zeus* after we've taken out the communications base. He'll tell them the position of the garrison and get our ships to blast it.'

'Right,' said Jake. 'And we give them a fixed time to stop the bombardment, so that we can move in while it's still in chaos and mop up the leftovers . . .'

'Like any fighters, choppers and any big guns,' nodded Zed.

'OK,' said Mick. 'Which do we go for first?'

'The three chopper sites,' said Pete. 'We wire them up with explosives on the ground, so if the enemy try to land, they'll blow themselves up. We can always clear the explosives before our own choppers need to use them. Then the next night we go for the communications base.'

'I think the communications base might have some nasties protecting it,' said Mick thoughtfully. 'There are two fences round it. I reckon the ground between the fences could well be mined.'

'In that case I suggest we hit it from a distance with a few missiles,' said Dobbs.

We all nodded in agreement.

'So, summing up,' said Mick, 'we do the chopper landing-sites the first night, the communications centre the second night and the garrison the third night.'

'Then, the invasion can start from dawn on the fourth day,' said Zed.

Chapter 11
SABOTAGE STRIKE

The next night we drew straws again to see who'd be left behind to look after our basecamp. Jake was excluded because he'd already done a turn. This time it was Zed who had to stay.

The rest of us kitted up and headed off towards the small hillside camp we'd called 'Enemy Special Forces' site.

The moon was bright, lighting up the hilltop and the four tents below it. The helipad was empty. Had the Huey taken off with the Special Forces? Or were they still there? We had no way of knowing.

We lay flat in the cover of a low mound of earth and I took a look at the camp through my night-glasses.

'There doesn't seem to be anyone on guard duty,' I whispered.

'That's because they don't know we're on

the island yet,' Frog whispered back. 'Once they do, all that will change.'

'I think we ought to go up and booby-trap the helipad first,' I suggested.

'Agreed,' said Frog. 'You and me, OK, Jerry?'

I nodded, and we gestured to the others to keep an eye on the tents.

Frog and I ran in a crouch to the hill, rifles ready as always and bags of grenades and wire slung over our shoulders.

We made it to the helipad with no trouble and immediately set to work. We pushed grenades into the earth in a grid pattern across the helipad, then looped wire between the pins of the grenades. When we'd finished it looked like a huge version of a cat's cradle game: a web of wire criss-crossing the hilltop. A helicopter landing would trigger the grenades as soon as it touched the wire.

We then hurried back to rejoin the others behind the mound.

'All done,' I said.

'OK,' said Mick. 'I suggest we shake their tree and see what falls out. So let's hit the big tent with an RPG. Anyone got a better idea?'

We shook our heads. If their Special Forces were there, we would be out-numbered. It made sense to open our attack like that, then react to whatever they came up with.

We unpacked the grenade-launcher, a Heckler & Koch 40-mm Granatpistole. Mick took aim with it and fired. A perfect shot. It disappeared right into the big tent, and a huge explosion of flame and smoke followed quickly.

We levelled our rifles, prepared to return fire if the enemy came out firing. But *nothing* happened. Literally, nothing.

Jake looked at me and frowned.

'They couldn't all have been in the big tent, surely? Mick can't have knocked them all out in one go,' he said.

Careful, in case there was a trap waiting for us, me, Jake, Mack and Dobbs moved towards the tents. Pete, Banco, Mick and Frog stayed behind the mound and kept us covered.

Me and Jake reached the big tent. Smoke and flames were pouring out of it. I turned on my torch and looked in. I could see that no one had been in the tent. The communications equipment had caught the blast of Mick's grenade and was now a mess of blackened, twisted metal and burning wires.

Mack and Dobbs moved swiftly to the three smaller tents. They were back within a minute.

'All empty,' said Mack. 'There's no one here. Just cases of stores.'

We looked at one another, puzzled. And then we shrugged. For some reason the Argentinians had evacuated this camp, but hadn't bothered to take their communications equipment and stores. Maybe they'd been too heavy to load into the Huey. Or maybe they had had to leave so fast that there hadn't been time to remove it.

More baffling was not even a guard had been left. It didn't make sense. Unless the camp had been closed for good, and the tents and equipment were to be picked up later.

'Oh well,' said Dobbs. He levelled his rifle at the smouldering communications equipment and let off a burst of bullets that finished it off altogether.

'No sense in leaving them a way to make contact when they get back,' he said.

* * *

93

We split into two groups to take out the helicopter landing-sites that Pete and Zed had spotted. Mick, Frog, Banco and Dobbs set off to deal with one, while me, Jake, Mack and Pete headed for the other.

Our landing-site was ten kilometres from the deserted hillside camp, so it took us a couple of hours to get to it. The bogs and marshes made progress slow. We wanted to keep in the shadows as we moved, but the terrain was flat and empty, so that was rarely possible. The bright moon meant we could be spotted easily. We wondered if the noise of the RPG and the gunfire during our attack on the camp had been heard. In open country noise can travel far.

We reached our target at 02.15 hours. This helipad was on a flat plain. There were three tents and a wooden shack next to it. Unlike the last site, these were occupied. In the moonlight I could see smoke coming from a short metal chimney poking through the roof of the shack. The dim glow from a lamp came through a crack in the flap of one of the tents.

The landing-site had a helicopter on it: a Mil Mi-24 like we'd blown up on Pebble

Island. It would have a crew of two and could carry up to eight soldiers. So, either we just had the crew here, or we also had a small unit of Argentinians.

'Let's do the same as we did before,' suggested Mack. 'Wire the helipad first with grenades, then hit the camp.'

We nodded.

This time me and Jake headed to the helipad with the grenades and wire, moving carefully all the time, trying not to make a noise.

We reached the wooden shack and listened. We could hear a faint hum and bursts of static. I mimed 'Radio' to Jake, and he nodded. There was a radio operator in there. I hoped he had his headphones firmly over his ears as he listened to the radio.

We moved on to the helipad and proceeded to push grenades into the earth round the Mi-24. Then we unrolled the wire and looped it from grenade pin to grenade pin.

'I think we ought to deal with the radio operator while we're here,' Jake whispered, as soon as we'd finished. 'Just in case action starts and he radios for help.'

'Good idea,' I whispered back.

We moved to the shack, rifles ready, skirting round the back of the three tents.

As we passed the first tent, I heard a faint metallic click. The next second a deafening fusillade poured from the tent.

Chapter 12
THE NEXT MOVE

I was saved by two things. First, after years of training and experience in the field, I reacted instinctively to the sound of that click, hurling myself to one side. The second thing that had saved me was the fact that the person inside the tent was firing blindly through the back at moonlit shadows.

Lying on the ground, I brought my rifle up and fired a burst into the tent. Jake, too, had reacted like me and was also flat on the ground, firing into the tent. Next, the whole area seemed to burst into gunfire. Lines of tracers of bullets tore through the bright moonlight from all directions. Out of the corner of my eye I saw a man appear and aim a pistol at me. I rolled and fired a burst which knocked him over.

As suddenly as it had started, it was all over. The noise of gunfire stopped. I got to my feet, wary, watching and preparing for another attack. But none came.

Mack and Pete had joined me and Jake.

'Anyone injured?' asked Mack.

I checked myself quickly. No burning sensation, no dull pain. Sometimes you can get shot and, because your body is pumping adrenalin so hard through your system, you don't even notice it at the time. I shook my head.

'No,' I said.

'I think I caught a ricochet,' said Jake, his hand to his face.

Pete took a look at him.

'You're lucky,' he said. 'It's only a flesh wound. Nothing serious.'

We checked the hut and the tents and the surrounding area.

We found four Argentinians. All dead.

'What about the chopper?' asked Mack, gesturing at the Mi-24. 'Destroy it or leave it?'

'I reckon we leave it,' I suggested. 'When the Argentinians turn up and see what's happened here, they'll either trigger the booby-traps on the helipad or find them and think the chopper is wired to blow as well. Also, when our blokes land, they might be able to use the chopper. We'll have to pass on word about the booby-traps so that none of our lot gets blown up.'

That was another thing about war – using equipment captured from the enemy. It had been that way for centuries. In the early days, warriors took their enemy's horses and used them. In the Second World War, each side used tanks seized from the enemy. Just change the markings and it was yours!

The others agreed with my suggestion about leaving the chopper, so we packed up and headed off back to our basecamp.

Banco, Dobbs, Frog and Mick were already there with Zed when we reached it. We filled them in on what had happened at our target.

'Same with us,' said Mick. 'Only the Argentinians jumped out while me and Frog were halfway through wiring up the helipad.'

'Three of them,' said Banco. 'Luckily, they were slow. And they all came from the same place. So me and Dobbs hit them and took them out.'

By now the night was ending and dawn was coming up. It was time to get some sleep. As always, we drew lots to see who took guard duty first: two on guard while the others slept. Pete and Dobbs drew first duty, me and Jake were lucky and drew the last shift, which meant we could get a good uninterrupted sleep.

As I crawled into my sleeping-bag I thought of the night's action. Seven Argentinian soldiers dead. No one in their right mind really likes killing, but that's war. If the Argentinians had been lucky, or better, it would have been us stretched out dead on the ground. And the Argentinians had started the whole thing by invading the Falklands. If you start a war, you have to take what's coming. If you don't like the heat, stay out of the kitchen. The main thing was we'd put three enemy helipads out of action. Tomorrow night we'd hit their communications base.

Jake and I took over watch duty at 11.00 hours. It was cold. Really cold. Not the kind of fresh cold that you get on a winter morning back in Britain, but a bitter icy cold. Even though it wasn't as cold here as it had been on South Georgia island, it was a reminder that we were in the South Atlantic, not far from the frozen Antarctic.

Despite the cold, this time we didn't light a fire. Our guess was that the Argentinians had discovered our night's work and would now be looking for us. They'd be using low-flying choppers over this part of the island. A small puff of smoke would give away our position. So we stayed in the cave and listened . . .

There was a chance that the Argentinians would think that the attacks had been done by Special Forces who had come in by chopper, done their job and then flown off. If so, then, provided their air search found no signs of us, they'd leave it at that. At least, that's what I hoped. After we hit the communications base, it would be a different story. Then they'd know for sure that we were on the island and they'd come looking for us.

The enemy helicopters came just after 14.00 hours. From the sound, there were two of them – a large one and a small one. We guessed the larger one was carrying assault troops, just in case we were spotted.

They circled over us for about ten minutes before continuing. So far, so good.

We spent the rest of the afternoon working out our plan of attack on the communications base. We assumed that security at the base would be stepped up after last night's events. More guards, both inside and out. Booby-traps.

'Because of the increased security, I think we ought to hit it from a distance,' I said. 'With missiles and mortars.'

'That'll be noisy,' said Pete. 'It'll draw attention to us.'

'Noise or no noise, it's got to be done. It's a key site. It's got to be wiped out. Let's face it, the Argentinians know we've been here and think we are probably still here, with other jobs to do. They're on alert.'

'I think Jerry's right,' said Mack. 'It's a job for missiles. We've got to take out the whole base – aerials, radios, the lot. The other good thing about a missile is it might fool the Argentinians into thinking it came from one of our ships or aircraft. Then they might think that last night was a one-off and that we've been choppered back to a ship.'

The others thought about this for a few seconds, and then nodded.

'Let's do it,' said Zed.

'OK,' said Frog. 'Time to sort out what we're taking with us.'

'Something big,' said Jake. 'Let's really make this look like an attack from offshore.'

Chapter 13
CASUALTY

We waited until 23.00 hours before setting off for the communications base. This time Pete had lost the draw and was left behind as guard.

We'd decided to hit the base first with mortars, followed by heavy armour-piercing grenades. Even if they didn't demolish it completely, they'd do serious damage.

Mick, Frog and Dobbs would be in charge of the L16 81-mm mortar. It's a great piece of kit, safe and reliable, especially for rapid firing.

Mack would be using the Brunswick RAW. This fits on a standard M16 rifle, converting it into a powerful grenade-launcher which can blow a hole over 30 cm across in a reinforced-concrete wall 20 cm thick.

I'd be using a 120-mm Sep DARD 120

rocket-launcher. You can take out a heavily armoured tank from the front with one of these.

Jake and Zed would be on back-up, rifles ready to deal with any opposition.

Once we'd hit the base, Banco would break radio silence to transmit the co-ordinates of the garrison to our ships offshore.

We'd be spread out for the attack, some near the base, others further away. If we were all bunched together, our chances of escape would be heavily reduced. Being spread out would improve them if things went wrong.

There was another reason for this: the weapons worked best at different ranges. The L16 mortar had a maximum range of 5,650 metres. The DARD 120 was only really effective up to 600 metres, and the Brunswick RAW was best within 200 metres. So we decided that Mick, Frog and Dobbs would set up the L16 4,000 metres from the base. I'd take up a position 500 metres from the target, with Jake as rifle back-up. Mack would be 200 metres from the target, and well away to one side of me, with Zed as his back-up.

Our signal to fire would be the first mortar dropping on to the base. As soon as it hit, me and Mack would open up. We'd keep up a sustained attack for two minutes and then shut down to allow Banco to send his radio transmission. Once Banco signalled this had been completed, we'd pack up and head back to our cave.

By the time we got to the target, it was just after midnight.

'Patrol,' whispered Jake, who was in the lead.

Immediately we all dropped to the ground and scanned the terrain ahead of us.

The communications base consisted of two buildings: a large one made from concrete blocks and a smaller brick-built one about fifty metres away. The large one was obviously for communications because its roof was covered with aerials and radar scanners. Both buildings were in a compound surrounded by two separate fences, each topped with razor wire.

There was one main gate into this compound, and a sentry stood on duty by it. He was wearing a steel helmet and carrying a rifle.

Just behind the sentry, I could see a dug-out with another soldier sitting behind a machine-gun on a tripod.

A vehicle like a quad bike had appeared from the small building. Through my night-glasses I could see an armed soldier behind the driver.

The vehicle trundled along at a slow speed, bumping over the uneven ground, to the door of the communications building. There it stopped and the soldier got off the back and went to the door. I saw him press a security key-pad with a sequence of numbers – the entry code – and then the door opened and he went in. The door slid shut behind him straight away.

From the reflection on the door of the lights along the inner and outer fences, I could tell it was made of metal.

The patrol vehicle turned and headed back to the smaller building.

'What's in that building?' I whispered to Frog.

'Me and Mick reckon it's a combined generator and storehouse,' Frog whispered back. 'We watched it for an hour when we were recce-ing.'

'That outer fence looks about one hundred metres from the main building,' said Mack. 'So I've got to get to a hundred metres of it. I'm going to have to do it from the side. I can't risk doing it from the front in case me and Zed are spotted by the sentry and machine-gunner.'

We nodded.

'Me and Jake will take a position on the left. You go on the right,' I said. 'That'll leave the mortar to handle the front.'

Mack nodded.

'OK, Zed,' he said. 'Let's go.'

Mack and Zed grabbed their ammo and the RAW and went off to the right-hand side of the perimeter fence.

Leaving Mick, Frog and Dobbs to set up the L16 and Banco to deal with the radio, Jake and I headed off to our position, me carrying the DARD 120 and one of the missiles, Jake bringing the other two missiles. The missiles for the DARD 120 are actually twice as heavy as the weapon itself, weighing in at 8.9 kg each as opposed to 4.5 kg for the launcher. Along with our regular rifles and ammo and grenades, we'd carried a lot of weight from the cave to here.

Jake and I reached our position and Jake lay flat, rifle covering the communications compound, while I prepared the launcher, loading the first missile.

The DARD 120 isn't a guided-missile system. Unlike some portable launchers, you don't lock on to your target and then let the missile fly until it hits home. The DARD 120 depends on the user getting the aim right.

Using the gun-sight, I aimed at a wall of the main building, some 500 metres away. Jake kept his eyes on the sentry at the main gate. So far he hadn't moved, except to march around for a few paces to keep himself warm against the cold.

I wondered if Mack and Zed were in position yet. They were the closest, and therefore the most vulnerable once the action started.

I crouched, eye pressed against the gun-sight, and waited, the launcher heavy on my shoulder.

'Come on, Mick,' I muttered under my breath. 'Hurry up. This thing weighs a tonne.'

It was as if the guys on the mortar had heard me, because suddenly there was a *WHOOMP!!* and a burst of flame from the mortar position in the night sky, and then the first mortar crashed on to the roof of the main building and blew the radar scanners to pieces.

Immediately the sentry and the machine-gunner opened up towards the mortar. At the same time I let go with the missile from the DARD 120. The launcher kicked back on my shoulder and the missile slammed into the main building's wall with such force that the wall disappeared in a huge cloud of dust. There was another explosion from the other side of the building, so I knew that Mack had also hit his target.

As I reloaded, Jake let fly with a burst of fire at the sentry-post.

Meanwhile, Mick, Frog and Dobbs were up to speed, their mortar shells raining down on the main building one after the other in a terrifying succession of ear-splitting explosions, flames and smoke.

I sent my second missile into the side of the small brick building, and it vanished in a cloud of swirling dust exploding outwards from it.

110

During all this, Mack was pumping grenade after grenade from the RAW into the main building. Mick, Frog and Dobbs also kept up their barrage of mortar shells. We were working like a well-oiled machine. Perfect team-work.

I put the final missile into the main building, which by now was a burning ball of fire, before signalling to Jake that it was time to go.

I picked up the DARD 120 and my rifle and headed back to where Mick, Frog and Dobbs were packing up the L16 and Banco was pulling down the aerial of the radio.

'Transmission completed,' said Banco.

Mack arrived, carrying the RAW.

'Zed's holding them off,' he said.

'Jake's doing the same on the other side,' I said.

As we were turning away from the chaos of the burning buildings, out of the corner of my eye I saw a tracer of bullets coming out from the compound, straight at Jake's position.

Just then, Zed joined us.

'Defensive fire,' he said. 'I think they might have hit Jake.'

'I'll go and see,' I said.

'I'll come with you,' said Mack. To the others, he said, 'Can you take the equipment?'

They nodded.

'OK,' he said. 'We'll see the rest of you back at the cave.'

Mack and I ran to where I'd left Jake. Tracers were still coming from the shattered compound, but they weren't aimed at anything in particular: the Argentinians were just firing blind, hoping to hit something.

Jake was lying on the ground when we reached him.

'My legs,' he grimaced. 'Some swine shot both of them.'

He'd been hit below the knees and blood was still pumping out.

'We'll fix you up properly as soon as we get back to the cave,' I said.

I pulled out a length of strapping I always keep with me and made a tourniquet round each of his legs, just above the knee, to try to stop the bleeding.

While I did this, Mack kept watch, in case the enemy came to attack us. But there was no sign of that happening: their hands were full trying to sort out the chaos we had created.

I hoisted Jake over my shoulder and then set off as fast as I could, with Mack beside me, rifle poised to fire as cover. I was lucky that Jake was fairly light. The ground was uneven and pitted with holes. The last thing I wanted was to put my foot in one of them and wrench my ankle, perhaps even fall and break it. Carrying Jake didn't help things.

The sound of gunfire from the compound had now ceased, to be replaced by the Argentinians yelling at each other in Spanish as they put out the fires.

As we slipped away, behind us the night sky was filled with smoke and sparks and flames. Job done.

Chapter 14
IN HIDING

Back at the cave, we started patching up Jake, working by the light of a lamp.

The big thing to watch out for if anyone's been shot, apart from stopping any bleeding, is the body going into shock. It can happen after the sort of severe loss of blood that Jake had suffered. Keeping the body warm helps to counter shock, so Mack piled some clothes on to Jake's upper body, while I cut away Jake's trousers from just above the knee, where I'd placed the tourniquets.

Next I gave Jake a shot of morphine to help numb the pain, and began examining his injuries.

The fibula (the long bone below the knee) of his left leg had been badly fractured in two places. He'd been luckier with his right leg: the bullets had torn out a piece of flesh from his calf, but the bones looked intact.

After loss of blood and shock, the next biggest danger is a wound becoming infected. So I cleaned all Jake's wounds as best I could. Afterwards I took a rest while Frog finished the job, making up and applying the dressings.

We made Jake as comfortable as we could on a makeshift bed at the back of the cave. Then we sorted out a guard rota and grabbed some sleep.

The next morning Jake was in a lot of pain, but he resisted any further injections of morphine, determined to deal with it himself.

'OK,' I told him, 'but if it gets too bad to handle, just let me know. One more shot isn't going to turn you into a junkie.'

'No, but the one after might,' grimaced Jake. 'I'll stay with the pain for as long as I can.'

I checked his temperature, which was holding steady at just over 98.6° F. Luckily for Jake, he was in great physical shape, which meant his body would heal quicker.

Then talk turned to last night's raid and what the Argentinians would do about it.

'They'll come looking for us,' said Frog.

'This time, one thing's for sure: they'll know it wasn't an attack from offshore.'

'It was every bit as good as!' grinned Mack. 'We brought those buildings down as surely as if a bomb had hit it. That'll mess up their communications for a while.'

'But it's going to make our attack on the garrison more difficult,' Pete said thoughtfully. 'They'll have patrols out, helicopters, everything – all trying to find us. We could run into them on our way to the garrison.'

'It's a chance we've got to take,' I said. 'We have to make sure the garrison is out of action by the time the main assault comes.'

For the rest of the day we stayed in the cave, keeping an eye on Jake and preparing for the fireworks that night. Banco had made radio contact with the *Zeus* and had been told that the bombardment would start at 03.00 hours and end at 04.00. A whole hour of heavy shelling raining down on the Argentinian garrison!

Then it would be up to us to move in and take out anything dangerous that had survived, so that the beach would be safe for our assault troops to land on.

Because we would split up inside the

activity as when Mack and I had made our first observation of it. Most of the enemy soldiers seemed to be in their quarters, asleep. There were guards on duty round the perimeter and patrols moving about inside the garrison itself.

The larger vehicles – the lorries and petrol tankers – had been parked up. There were two aircraft by the landing-strip: a Mirage fighter and an Alouette helicopter.

A series of machine-gun posts had been set up along the beach, so the Argentinians were obviously expecting an attack from the sea. Or maybe they were just being careful.

The seven of us lay there, watching and waiting, the time creeping round to 03.00 ours.

The bombardment began exactly on hedule. The first we, or the Argentinians, ew about it was when shells started pping right in the centre of the garrison a series of explosions ripped it apart. of the first shells landed smack on the ette, leaving a huge crater in the nd where it had stood. Another shell d a direct hit on the Mirage. Both ft were blown to smithereens.

sound was so loud that even in our

garrison, we decided that one of us would send up a flare as the signal to withdraw. Then we'd beat a fighting retreat away from the garrison and hope that some of the Argentinians would follow us, weakening the resistance our guys would face.

We drew lots for who would fire the flare and Banco got the job.

'Make sure you give us enough time to make some serious impact on their defences,' Pete told Banco.

'But don't leave it too long,' added Zed. 'We don't want to give them time to bring in reinforcements against us.'

'Trust me, lads,' said Banco. Then he gave a smirk. 'How does this flare thing work, by the way?'

About half a dozen times during the day we heard the sound of helicopters flying low and passing backwards and forwards over the cave. A major search for us was obviously under way.

'I'm tempted to knock them down with the DARD if they come over again,' said Dobbs after the sixth time we heard them.

The camouflage webbing hid the cave's entrance from the air. However, we weren't sure if it would deceive the prying eyes of a shore patrol. Luckily, none passed by.

Darkness fell. I checked the dressings on Jake's wounds. I was worried because his temperature had gone up and I could see from the sweat on his face that he was in great pain.

'Don't worry, mate,' I told him. 'We'll soon have you back on board the *Zeus*.'

My watch ticked round until finally it was 23.00 hours. Time for us to go.

Although the offshore bombardment wasn't due to begin until 03.00 hours, we knew it would take us at least three hours to reach the garrison, especially if we ran into Argentinian patrols.

This time Mack was staying behind to guard the cave and look after Jake.

Me, Mick, Frog, Dobbs, Banco, Pete and Zed set off. We travelled light, taking just our M16 rifles, pistols, ammo and knives. The damage tonight would be done by our ships' heavy guns. Just in case we might need something with a bit of punch, Mick brought the RAW attachment with him and we all carried our share of grenades for it. This was going to be the big one.

Chapter 15
INVASION

As on all our missions here, we trav off-road and off-track, over rough boggy ground. We'd decided that w less likely to run into the enemy o type of terrain. It made for travelling, but it was probably didn't want to get into a fire-figh enemy before we'd reached our

By 02.00 hours we were in p of a hillock about a couple o from the Argentinian garris were out of range of the en of our own gunners. The g ships always claim the accurate, but I've known astray by at least 100 didn't want to be hit by

Through my night-g that the garrison was

distant position it was difficult to talk to one another.

Mick pointed out to sea.

'*Look!*' he shouted.

It wasn't only the garrison that was being bombarded, but the Argentinian ships lying at anchor. Shells were dropping down on them and we could see fires starting on their decks. The bombardment would also have started on the other landing points, at Goose Green and Bluff Cove.

The noise was incredible, and so was the vibration. Even here, two kilometres away, the ground shook from the impact of the ships' shells.

The enemy soldiers tried to take cover, but there was no escaping this amazing bombardment.

Right before our eyes, machine-gun posts disappeared, vehicles burst into flames, buildings disintegrated and clouds of smoke, dust and debris covered the garrison.

Yet still the shells came. It was hard to think that anyone or anything would be standing afterwards.

As 04.00 hours approached, we took stock of the situation. Through all the smoke we could see that some of the enemy guns had indeed survived the onslaught and were still in action.

As suddenly as it had started, the bombardment ceased – spot on 04.00 hours.

Everything was eerily quiet.

'OK,' said Pete. 'Let's go.'

We ran down the hillock, spread out in a line, crouching low. At this distance darkness still hid us. For the moment the Argentinians were more concerned with sorting out the mess than preparing for an attack from inland. The bombardment had been so fierce that I could see many of the enemy soldiers walking around in a daze, shocked by what had happened.

By the time Frog and I reached the perimeter of the garrison, the enemy were beginning to pull themselves together. A petrol tanker was being driven away from the flames. The driver spotted us, halted, raised his rifle and fired at us. I returned fire as Frog lobbed a grenade into tanker's cab. We had thrown ourselves flat on the ground by the time the grenade exploded. The cab burst into a raging ball of fire. Seconds later, the tanker blew up in a huge glare of yellow and red flame.

garrison, we decided that one of us would send up a flare as the signal to withdraw. Then we'd beat a fighting retreat away from the garrison and hope that some of the Argentinians would follow us, weakening the resistance our guys would face.

We drew lots for who would fire the flare and Banco got the job.

'Make sure you give us enough time to make some serious impact on their defences,' Pete told Banco.

'But don't leave it too long,' added Zed. 'We don't want to give them time to bring in reinforcements against us.'

'Trust me, lads,' said Banco. Then he gave a smirk. 'How does this flare thing work, by the way?'

About half a dozen times during the day we heard the sound of helicopters flying low and passing backwards and forwards over the cave. A major search for us was obviously under way.

'I'm tempted to knock them down with the DARD if they come over again,' said Dobbs after the sixth time we heard them.

The camouflage webbing hid the cave's entrance from the air. However, we weren't sure if it would deceive the prying eyes of a shore patrol. Luckily, none passed by.

Darkness fell. I checked the dressings on Jake's wounds. I was worried because his temperature had gone up and I could see from the sweat on his face that he was in great pain.

'Don't worry, mate,' I told him. 'We'll soon have you back on board the *Zeus*.'

My watch ticked round until finally it was 23.00 hours. Time for us to go.

Although the offshore bombardment wasn't due to begin until 03.00 hours, we knew it would take us at least three hours to reach the garrison, especially if we ran into Argentinian patrols.

This time Mack was staying behind to guard the cave and look after Jake.

Me, Mick, Frog, Dobbs, Banco, Pete and Zed set off. We travelled light, taking just our M16 rifles, pistols, ammo and knives. The damage tonight would be done by our ships' heavy guns. Just in case we might need something with a bit of punch, Mick brought the RAW attachment with him and we all carried our share of grenades for it. This was going to be the big one.

Chapter 15
INVASION

As on all our missions here, we travelled off-road and off-track, over rough and boggy ground. We'd decided that we were less likely to run into the enemy over this type of terrain. It made for harder travelling, but it was probably safer. We didn't want to get into a fire-fight with the enemy before we'd reached our target.

By 02.00 hours we were in place, on top of a hillock about a couple of kilometres from the Argentinian garrison. There we were out of range of the enemy as well as of our own gunners. The gunners on our ships always claim their shooting is accurate, but I've known many shells go astray by at least 100 metres, and we didn't want to be hit by one of them.

Through my night-glasses I could see that the garrison was at the same level of activity as when Mack and I had made our first observation of it. Most of the enemy soldiers seemed to be in their quarters, asleep. There were guards on duty round the perimeter and patrols moving about inside the garrison itself.

The larger vehicles – the lorries and petrol tankers – had been parked up. There were two aircraft by the landing-strip: a Mirage fighter and an Alouette helicopter.

A series of machine-gun posts had been set up along the beach, so the Argentinians were obviously expecting an attack from the sea. Or maybe they were just being careful.

The seven of us lay there, watching and waiting, the time creeping round to 03.00 hours.

The bombardment began exactly on schedule. The first we, or the Argentinians, knew about it was when shells started dropping right in the centre of the garrison and a series of explosions ripped it apart. One of the first shells landed smack on the Alouette, leaving a huge crater in the ground where it had stood. Another shell scored a direct hit on the Mirage. Both aircraft were blown to smithereens.

The sound was so loud that even in our

Frog and I got to our feet and moved into the garrison. All around us there was the sound of gunfire. Our unexpected arrival from the darkness had clearly created panic in an already confused situation. The Argentinians were running round like headless chickens again, not knowing where we'd strike them next. The seven of us spread out so that we could wreak havoc on the whole garrison. We'd decided that each of us would chose a target, let off a burst, disappear round the corner and pop up somewhere else and look for another target to knock out.

The target I'd picked out for myself was a machine-gun post overlooking the beach.

Its two crew were still in position and I waited till I was nearly on them before I let them have a burst of gunfire. They both crumpled and toppled over. Then I fired into the machine-gun itself, smashing the works and putting it out of action. That'd be one machine-gun less for our lads to face when dawn came up.

I ducked and dived around the garrison, making use of any available cover – wrecked lorries, stacks of oil drums, crates. I hit everything that could be used against our invasion. I knew the other lads would be doing the same.

I don't know how long I'd been doing this when the flare went up, a green cascade lighting up the sky above us – Banco's signal to withdraw.

Immediately I headed for the perimeter, firing off a burst from my M16 as I did so, just to keep the enemy at bay.

We'd agreed that the hillock where we'd started from would also be our RV point and I headed for it now. As I ran, bullets whistled into the darkness, narrowly missing me. I stopped, turned and let off a burst in the direction of the garrison. Then I started to run again, zigzagging as I went. Just when I thought I was safe, the darkness was lit up by the blinding glare of a searchlight from inside the garrison. It swept round, catching me in its beam like a rabbit caught in a car's headlights.

I cursed and threw myself into a ditch as a hail of bullets poured over my head and into the earth in front me.

Suddenly there was an explosion. The searchlight went out and all was blackness again.

I heard a sound near me. I swung round,

bringing my rifle up, but it was only Mick, holding the RAW grenade-launcher. I could see his white teeth form a huge grin in his blackened face.

'Nearly had you then!' he laughed. He patted the RAW. 'Lucky I had my friend with me. Popped a grenade smack in the centre of the searchlight.'

'Good thing you did,' I said. 'Any sign of the others?'

Just then Banco joined us, followed by Frog, Dobbs and Pete. Zed arrived last of all. I was relieved that we hadn't suffered any casualties on this mission.

'All present and correct,' said Dobbs. 'I think we ought to get out of here.'

'Let's give them a final present,' said Mick as he fired off another grenade from the RAW launcher into the garrison.

A series of bursts of rapid gunfire came from the garrison, followed by the sound of engines starting up. Next we saw headlights heading our way.

'All terrain vehicles,' said Zed. 'They're after us.'

'Cat and mouse,' said Frog. 'And we're the mice. Right, lads, break-up time.'

We had agreed that if the Argentinians

took the bait and tailed us, we'd split into two groups: me, Mick and Banco would head in one direction; Frog, Dobbs, Pete and Zed in another. This reduced the chance of them getting all of us.

'Head for the high ground,' said Banco. 'The ATVs will have difficulty getting up it.'

'It makes us easier targets, though,' Mick pointed out.

We began climbing up the rock-face nearby. I could hear the ATVs quite clearly now. They were getting nearer and nearer.

Banco got to the top first. In the dim light that was starting to filter through the dawn sky, I saw Banco turn and fire off a burst at a spot behind me.

There was a loud crash.

I pulled myself up over the edge of the rock-face and then gave Mick a hand-up. As I did so I took a quick look down.

Banco had hit the driver of the leading ATV. The driver had lost control and swerved into a rocky outcrop. The ATV behind it had stopped to sort out the mess.

Me, Mick and Banco lay on the ground and poured rifle fire down on to the enemy soldiers, forcing them to take cover behind their vehicles.

By now it was dawn. I looked across the wreckage of the enemy garrison towards the beach. There were specks in the sea, hundreds of them, getting larger and larger. Assault craft. The invasion force was coming in!

The Argentinian soldiers from the ATVs had also spotted our guys. They stood up, their hands held in the air in surrender.

While Banco and Mick went down to take them prisoner, I trained my binoculars on the beach and watched our blokes arrive.

It was a magnificent sight to see: 5,000 of our paratroopers and Commandos, coming off the boats and storming up the beach, the men in front firing as they went.

Last night's naval bombardment, followed by our attack, had taken the fight out of the Argentinians, and I could see groups of them surrendering to our troops. It was over. We'd won.

HISTORICAL NOTE

Although this book is fiction, it is based on events that actually happened.

On Friday 19 March 1982 some Argentinian scrap-dealers did land at the derelict whaling-station at Leith, South Georgia island, and raise the Argentinian flag. There was a British Antarctic Survey (BAS) team based there. It reported the incident to the Governor of the Falkland Islands, Sir Rex Hunt, in Port Stanley, 1,400 kilometres away on East Falkland island. Hunt told the leader of the BAS team, who was also the Magistrate of South Georgia, that the Argentinians must get his permission to fly their flag. The Argentinians refused to do this. (The Falklands had been under British sovereignty since 1833, but Argentina had long-standing claims over them.)

The Argentinian government ordered the ice-breaker *Bahia Paraiso*, with a large force of Marines on board, to sail to South Georgia to 'protect' the scrap-dealers. At the same time a small party of British Marines left East Falkland for South Georgia.

On 25 March, the Argentinian Marines landed on South Georgia. On 2 April, Argentinian forces invaded the Falkland Islands.

Britain and Argentina were now at war.

A task force was assembled in Britain and sent to the South Atlantic to recover the Falkland Islands.

After a series of battles against overwhelming odds, the British Marines on South Georgia were forced to surrender. Meanwhile, more Argentinian forces poured on to the Falkland Islands.

The first step by the British was the retaking of South Georgia, code-named Operation Paraquat. A party of men from SAS D Squadron went ashore in three helicopters in appalling conditions on 21 April. Under cover of a bombardment from HMS *Antrim*, they launched attacks on the Argentinian positions at the two harbours of Leith and Grytviken. The Argentinians eventually surrendered on 26 April. (These events were the basis for another book in this series, *Hostile Terrain*.)

The British task force arrived at the Falkland Islands on 29 April. From that date the SAS carried out secret raids on Argentinian outposts and bases, including an attack on Pebble Island on 14 May in which they destroyed all the enemy aircraft there.

The SAS then continued to launch further covert attacks on Argentinian positions on East Falkland, weakening the Argentinian defences in preparation for the main assault by the British.

On 27 May British Commandos and paratroopers landed on the Falklands and the next day defeated enemy forces at the Battle of Goose Green. The British assault continued throughout late May and the beginning of June.

On 11 June the battle for Port Stanley began. On 13 June came the crucial battle for Mount Tumbledown. It was captured by 2 Scots Guards. Meanwhile, 2 Para captured Wireless Ridge, the Gurkhas took Mount William and the Welsh Guards claimed Sapper Hill.

The Argentinians fled from these positions into Port Stanley and began surrender negotiations.

During this final series of battles, 40 British personnel were killed and 120 wounded. The actual figures for killed and wounded Argentinians are not known. However, their losses were heavier than the British losses. (Argentinian forces in and around Port Stanley numbered approximately 8,500.)

The Argentinians surrendered on 14 June.

The final casualty figures for the whole Falklands War were: 237 British armed forces personnel killed (plus 18 civilians) and 759 wounded; 746 Argentinians killed and an unknown number wounded.

OBSERVATION PATROL

Being on observation patrol (OP) is one of the most vital and dangerous areas of work that the SAS carries out. A four-man team is inserted behind enemy lines, either by parachute, by sea or by land over a border. Once behind enemy lines, the team's job is to report back on the enemy's positions, strength, weapons — in fact, everything that can be found out about the enemy. With this information, the most effective kind of attack can be mounted.

It is dangerous work because there is always the risk of being caught. To avoid being detected, there are certain basic rules: do not be heard, seen or smelt.

1. Do not use soap or perfumed cosmetics, because these will be detected by the enemy.
2. Do not cook food unless your position is absolutely safe, because a fire will also be detected — either visually, when the smoke is seen, or from the smell of the smoke, which can be detected some distance away.
3. Avoid using existing roads or tracks.
4. Keep away from areas where people live (unless the surveillance is in an urban area).
5. Check your approach route for tracks from other people.

6. Prepare an escape route.
7. Sleep in full gear, including boots, ready for a quick getaway.

THE HIDE

The hide must blend in totally with the surrounding area. Use naturally occurring hiding-places (caves, rocky outcrops, over-hangs, etc.) and, if needed, add to them using camouflage.

OBSERVATION EQUIPMENT

1. Binoculars, telescopes, periscopes — to suit the environment.
2. Night-vision equipment.
3. Infra-red laser projectors. Targets can be marked for attack by aircraft. This is done with lasers. They project marks that are invisible to the naked eye on to buildings, but the marks can be spotted by suitably equipped aircraft.
4. Thermal-imagers. These identify heat generated by a human body — picking out the presence of someone even when they cannot be seen with the naked eye because they are hidden (e.g. behind a snow bank).

SAS SURVIVAL KIT

The survival kit must be as small as possible so that it can be carried around easily and not be a burden. Only absolutely essential items should be included. It should be kept in a waterproof container. The items included in a survival kit will depend on the particular preferences of the user and the kind of conditions he will be exposed to, but a basic kit would probably include the following:

WATER-PURIFICATION TABLETS

These will kill harmful bacteria in dirty water. Each tablet will purify a litre of water in ten minutes.

SURVIVAL BAG

This is a large windproof and waterproof polythene bag to prevent frost-bite and hypo-thermia. It can also be used to collect water.

FLINT AND STEEL

These are used for lighting a fire in all kinds of weather.

ALL-WEATHER MATCHES

Sometimes these are preferred to a flint and steel. They are waterproof and windproof. When struck, they burn for up to twelve seconds and they won't go out, even underwater. However, you can run out of them — something that doesn't happen to a flint and steel.

CANDLES

A 10-cm candle will give light for up to three hours. Candles made from animal fat can also be eaten in an emergency.

TAMPON

The best tinder for lighting a fire comes from the cotton in a tampon.

CONDOM

This is the best way to carry water. It has a capacity of 1.5 litres when filled. Preferably use something like a sock to cover the condom to help support the weight of the water.

COMPASS

NEEDLE

Take one with a large eye for thread strong enough for sewing heavy materials, such as leather or canvas. The needle can also be magnetized for use as a compass needle.

KNIFE

A pocket knife with foldaway blades is best.
The multi-purpose Swiss Army knife is ideal.

STRONG CORD

A long length of strong cord has many uses.
The best sort is parachute cord, which is
extremely strong. It is made of an outer
layer braided together over a thinner inner
cord. The inner cord can be taken out and
used as thread or as a fishing line.

MEDICAL KIT

- assorted wound dressings (plasters and
  bandages)
- butterfly sutures (to hold edges of wounds
  together)
- antibiotics
- pain-relief tablets
- antihistamine cream (for insect bites and
  allergies)